SURGEONS OF TERROR II

SURGEONS OF TERROR II

RON WOOTTERS

"Surgeons of Terror II," by Ron Wootters. ISBN 1-58939-824-6.

Published 2005 by Virtualbookworm.com Publishing Inc., P.O. Box 9949, College Station, TX 77842, US. ©2005, Ron Wootters. All rights reserved. No part of this publication may be reproduced, stored in a retrieval system, or transmitted in any form or by any means, electronic, mechanical, recording or otherwise, without the prior written permission of Ron Wootters.

Manufactured in the United States of America.

TO ROSEMARY, JOAN, EDNA AND CLARENCE(SLIM)

IN MEMORY OF

Andy, Friend and one of my Judo Instructors.

LT. Colonel McDonald, USMC Cuba 1960 - 1962
Marine Barracks Executive Officer.

In real life they have gone on ahead to perform recon.

Ronald Randolph (Pitt), My friend

Mr. Enoeda (Tora), one of my Karate Instructors.

Sid Smith, Friend, Washington, D.C. 1967 – 1977
S/Sgt Clarence(Teddy)Smith, Original 5307th
1944 Merrill's Marauders - Present day 75th Ranger Regiment

SPECIAL THANKS TO

Milt Kemble, Larry Scheetz and Carol Di Salvi for reading the
manuscript and giving their honest opinions.

Lisa D'Angelo, BookInk.com, for editing the original manuscript
and for her opinion and advice.

LT. Colonel J.H. (Pat) Carothers, USMC (ret), for reviewing the
manuscript and for his corrections, opinion and advice.

SPECIAL THANKS TO THE MEDICAL COMMUNITY

David DiPietro,   M.D. Family Practice
Paul Spiro,   M.D. Family Practice
Joseph Curci,   M.D. General Surgery & idea for title.
Michael Mooradd,   M.D. Cardiology
Steven Guidera,   M.D. Cardiology
Randy Metcalf,   M.D. Cardiothoracic Surgery
James H. Wright   M.D. Anesthesiology
Robert O'Connor   M.D. Anesthesiology
Joseph Shrager,   M.D. Dermatology
Steven Flashner,   M.D. Urology
Melchiore Vernace,   M.D. Nephrology
Timothy Orphanides,   M.D. Gastroenterology
Les Szekely,   M.D. Pulmonary Disease
Robert Linkenheimer,   D.O. Emergency Medicine
Mark Choi,   M.D. Emergency Medicine
Mark Bydalek,   D.M.D Dentistry

Mr. Rich Reif, Physician Assistant's, Nurses, Staff, Labs and the Cardiac Rehab Center at Doylestown Hospital.

Rosemary and I are very fortunate to live in an area where we have access to such excellent medical care.

PROLOGUE

It was early spring in Caan, France and the evenings were starting to get warmer with the aid of mild breezes blowing in off the Mediterranean Sea. There was not much activity along the water front tonight as two men in casual attire walked past the small bars and clubs at that end of town.

The two continued their conversation, about how the Riviera had changed over the years, as they crossed the street to continue their walk on a pier that extended out into the small harbor. Boats and yachts were backed up to the pier side-by-side, each being secured to the pier with its own lines.

With the exception of the three people, in what amounted to a small floating bar halfway up the pier, everything was very quiet. The two men admired the boats as they continued their walk.

When they got to the end of the pier, the Frenchmen started to refill his pipe as the Russian reached for another cigarette. As smoke filled the air the only thing that could be heard were the sounds of gentle waves as they splashed against the pier and the boats.

Satisfied that his pipe was lit the Frenchman broke the silence with a question. "Have you made a decision on my business proposition?"

The Russian took a deep breath before answering. "The items you require will be very difficult to obtain."

The Frenchman shook his head in agreement as he took a draw on his pipe.

"I am not saying it is impossible," the Russian continued, "especially with the economy in a shambles, but it will require much planning and careful execution."

"That shouldn't be a problem for you, Boris," quipped the Frenchman, "Back in your KGB day you drove the West nuts with some of your projects."

1

"I was lucky Rene'," Boris quickly replied.

Modesty wasn't the usual thing one got when talking with a Russian, but then Boris was far from the usual.

"There is another thing," Boris added, "I'll require an additional fifty thousand dollars. I hear the prices are going up in the technical sell-out department."

The Frenchman again shook his head without hesitation.

The Russian looked a little puzzled and questioned why the Frenchman was agreeing without question.

"I'm just a go between of a go between," Rene' stated. "For my part I am being paid very well, and having been around for many years, get the feeling if we are straightforward and honest with these people everything will be okay. If not, they will probably kill us. It's our choice."

After a brief silence the two continued discussing the financial arrangements, Swiss accounts, and contact information. The meeting they had earlier in the day covered all of the other requirements.

When all of the items had been covered the two men paused to again light up their smokes.

As Rene' exhaled he remarked, "It looks like it's back into the business for you."

"For the last time," Boris replied. "It's retirement after this one."

"Are you set financially for retirement?" asked Rene'.

"I'll make do," Boris replied.

"I'm sure you could make do better if you had more funds," Rene' suggested.

"Am I going to hear additional conditions on the dealings we are transacting," Boris said with a little hostility in his voice.

"No, no," Rene' insisted, "we have completed our dealings on that matter."

"I know you're not inquiring about my available funds for nothing," Boris said.

"Well, now that you mention it," Rene' admitted, "I have been authorized to approach you about another matter for say about three times the amount you are getting for this deal."

"When I told you about my retirement, I didn't mean under a

tombstone," Boris informed Rene'. "For that amount of money it will be something very, very dangerous."

"I know what you're saying," Rene' agreed, as he put his hand on Boris' left shoulder, "but let's talk about it as we walk."

CHAPTER ONE

The cover story that the Barn and House had been converted into a very exclusive bed and breakfast, with no reservations available until the year 2009, seemed to be holding up still.

During the teams absence JJ had some renovations done on the property and things were pretty busy for awhile.

Joe Altvater and his four sons made some needed repairs to the barns roof and Dan Di Salvi doubled the size of the Com shack. Tony Denise & Company added downstairs bed & bath rooms to the main house while John Hoff's group attended to the plumbing needs and Fred Nanni the electrical requirements.

Bob & Dawn Bell painted the additions and after a quick sniff around by Heidi Bell, the K-9 contingent was satisfied and renovations were considered completed.

Good work done by good people.

After inspection JJ was very pleased with the renovations and was looking out the new window in the com shack when his thoughts again returned to a continuing worry, the formation of the Board and the Team. His personal feelings about the need for a group to fight terrorism outside of government control remained the same, but the fact he had gotten others involved at great risk to themselves bothered him constantly.

The men he handpicked for the Board had the same feelings and had reassured him when he expressed his concerns, but the worry remained.

With several projects successfully completed JJ started feeling a little better about forming the group, but if the huge project that was in its initial planning stage got approved by the Board / Team the potential for disastrous results were extremely high.

The Team was again in residence at the Barn. After their last project everyone was given a few months off primarily for their excellent performance and partly due to the project taking place on U.S. soil. Dispersing the Team until things cooled down seemed to be a good idea.

JJ and General Mac were attending the first Team meeting since they returned and were presenting a project for their consideration. At the end of the presentation the Team members looked at each other, shook their heads, laughed, and immediately started firing questions at JJ and Mac.

"Do you realize how much planning and time will be involved for something like this?"

"We do," answered Mac, "and if in the middle of planning we hit a problem that is too big, we will scrap the entire project."

"Last count there were only ten of us?"

"Yes," JJ replied, "and we totally understand if you turn this one down."

"If we take on this Project will it be the one and only one until it is completed?"

"Yes," JJ answered, "and the Board also feels due to the importance of this project, the use of any additional resources will not be a problem."

After about ten more questions JJ took back control of the meeting and announced, "I think maybe this project is a little too ambitious for a group this size."

"Hold on," JC interrupted. "This project is huge, but we just want to make sure you and the other Board members realize how much time, planning, and resources will be involved."

"Believe me, we do," JJ answered.

"I hope so," added Blue Jay. "When we were planning the Cuba project some big shot was running around here acting like a spanked ass."

"I remember him," added Mac. "He was all concerned about how things were being run."

"Okay, okay," JJ conceded, "I promise I'll stay out of your planning from now on."

"I think we will have to kick this one around for a while before we give a yes or no," JC stated.

5

"Understood," JJ acknowledged, "Take as much time as you need."

A few more issues were covered then the meeting was adjourned.

The following morning JJ and Mac were at the office in New York City talking with the new member of the Board, retired Admiral Fox or Foxie as General Mac liked to call him. The Admiral didn't know the other Board members, but got unanimous approval from them due to his major contribution during the last Project. At the time he was unaware of what was going on, but after a quick analysis made a move that defused a situation and enabled the Project to come to a normal completion. At the time Admiral Fox was on active duty and due to retire in a few months. JJ and Mac tried and were successful in recruiting him with a starting date of after his retirement.

When all of the Board members had arrived everyone went into the boardroom for formal introductions and to bring Foxie up to speed on the organization and the Team.

With everyone seated, JJ brought the meeting to order.

"The first thing on the agenda will be the introduction of our new member, Admiral Fox," JJ announced. "I'll just do a quick intro around the table and we can talk in more detail when we take a coffee break."

With that said JJ started introductions down the left side of the table. "I think you know this guy?" JJ quipped as he motioned towards General Mac.

"Yeah, I've seen him around once or twice," the Admiral confirmed.

Seated to Mac's left was John Howard, president of Zerk Pharmaceutical Company, Jeff Dawson, president of International Oil, Gil Dunn, current president of Van Corcoven Firearms Company, and Charles Wilson, president of Wilson Explosives Company.

Admiral Fox acknowledged each man as he was introduced and offered a firm handshake.

"Admiral Fox," Gil Dunn announced, "that was a nice catch you made in D.C."

"Thank you," the Admiral replied, "It was a good thing I saw Blue Jay through the window of the jet when I took Mac to the air strip that night or I wouldn't have intervened between him and the police officers."

"By the way, Mac, that reminds me, who gave you the okay to use my base at Gitmo to hide after the theatrics in Cuba?"

"Theatrics?" Mac perks up. "See, that's what I get for trying to be nice. I just happened to be in the area and decided to pay my old buddy a visit. Is it my fault a team of ruffians got stranded at Gitmo and needed a ride?"

"And what is this, Admiral Fox this and Admiral Fox that? He's Foxie," Mac added.

"Do you prefer Foxie?" JJ inquired.

"My friends call me that," the Admiral replied, "and I think everyone at this table can call me Foxie, except maybe Mac."

Everyone at the table smiled as they realized Foxie would fit right in with their group.

"Since Mac has brought up the subject," JJ announced, "let me introduce the ruffians to you."

JJ stood and moved to the tripod at the front of the room and prepared to start the list. "The original charter allows for no contact between the Board and the Team members." JJ started, "We have had a few blips on the radar scope in that department, but it is still intact. Mac and myself serve as the liaison and attend both Board and Team meetings."

"For security reasons we feel the Team and Board members do not require knowledge of each other's identities. If needed, the Team can communicate through Mac or myself. The Board initiates the projects and requires more knowledge of the Team and their abilities so we have developed a code name and abilities type of information brief for each Team member and I will give you a very high overview of the Team members," JJ informed the Admiral.

"If I go into details and accomplishments we will be here all day."

With that said, JJ started the list, "JC, team leader, retired

Colonel. Marine Corps, pilot, expert with weapons and our main gizmo man.

"Blue Jay, field team leader, contract type, prior to that Marine Corps, & CIA."

"I've met Blue Jay," the Admiral interrupted.

"That's right," JJ smiled, "how could I have forgotten that?"

"I hope you don't hold that against us," Gil Dunn announced, "The kid has been a pain in my ass since, forever."

As the Admiral looked in Dunn's direction, JJ inquired,

"Gil, aren't you the one that suggested we consider Blue Jay for the Team."

"I take the fifth on that one," Gil answered, "and if I did it must have been when my malaria was acting up."

Foxie could tell by the reactions of the other Board members there are a lot of humorous stories to be told about Gil Dunn and Blue Jay.

JJ took control back and continued the list, "Bean, part-time contractor type, prior Army Special Forces, Airborne Ranger, CIA. Benz, Japanese, heavy in martial arts, been in the contract business many years. Panda, Philippino, also martial arts, takes on contracts from time to time. Regular occupation engineering consultant. Check, Arab, explosives, takes on contracts from time to time, owns a Middle East restaurant. Tic, Cuban, explosives, takes on contracts from time to time, stock broker. Bris, French, primarily a contractor, but also is an Artist and a good one. Pru, English, contractor, long range shooter. Met, German, also a contractor, long range shooter. And Air Jockey, contractor, can fly helicopters, most prop aircraft, the corporate jet and able to function as a Team member on the ground if needed."

"JC has done an excellent job in putting this Team together," JJ said with pride, "He selected all of these men for their experience, skills, and integrity, plus a big part of the language area is covered. As you can see by their nationalities we have six languages covered and Bean can speak a few languages from the old Soviet block countries. In addition to speaking the languages the individuals can also fit into a situation where that language is spoken. He also doubled up in specialties where possible. Long-range shooters, Martial Arts, and so on, and JC is the backup to the pilot and in other areas."

"They look good on paper and we have found out through experience even better when they are on a project."

"I have to agree with that," Foxie offered, "I know they kicked a gang of asses on that Cuba project."

"Since you brought up the Cuba project Admiral," JJ inquires, "are you aware of any Cuban Freedom Fighters operating in the area of the base? They seem to have been the benefactors of some very expensive weapons."

The Admiral looked puzzled until he noticed Mac looking toward the ceiling, then he realized Mac must have been bullshiting JJ. Before Foxie could start dancing that fine line between truth and not so true, Mac saved him the trouble.

"Okay JJ, you got me, it wasn't Cuban Freedom Fighters," Mac confessed, "it was the Cuban Mob. I was afraid you would get upset if you knew the Team gave the weapons to Charley Tuna's gang for helping them get out of harm's way."

"Didn't we cover this topic before?" John Howard asked.

"I believe we did," Jeff Dawson confirmed, "maybe Foxie would like to hear about the projects?"

JJ looked at Howard & Dawson and gave them a, "nice try sports' fans," then turned back to Mac and inquired, "How in the fuck did you come up with that story?"

Mac leaned back from the table, extended his hands with palms up and proclaimed, "The truth is where you find it."

"Unfortunately in your case it usually stays in the lost and found department," JJ replied. "The Cuban Mob," JJ said shaking his head while letting out a laugh he could no longer hold in. "Are we ready for a coffee break?" With the Board in agreement everyone adjourns to the back of the room for coffee.

Over an hour had passed since the coffee break started and the new member had been the center of attention. The Board members started by asking Foxie questions and a short time later the conversations changed to exchanging ideas and opinions. It looked like Foxie was well on his way to becoming a part of this group.

JJ checked his watch and realized it was time to reconvene the meeting. "Excuse me gentlemen, I think it's time to continue the meeting."

All members acknowledged JJ's suggestion and returned to their seats.

"Foxie, there is another group I would like to tell you about, House Staff," JJ began. "When JC started recruiting the Team, Mac started recruiting people that could cook, keep house, and also act as security for the home base, especially when the Team was away."

"Mac got in contact with a retired Marine Corps First Sergeant, code name Top, who in turn recruited two women that used to be Field Agents in the Intelligence Community. Their code names are LadyA and Lady1 or is it the other way round?"

"I don't mind telling you, Mac and I had a hell of a time coming up with code names for the ladies that they would accept," JJ admitted as Mac chuckled remembering the episode.

"Don't get me wrong, they are all first class and have proven it both in their primary duties and when they all volunteered for an emergency Project that was extremely dangerous. They are all first class professionals that can be counted on."

"At this point," JJ continued, "I will give the Admiral an overview of the current Project. With his background and experience I am sure his opinion will be welcomed."

Thirty minutes later JJ was asking the Admiral for his opinion.

"I hope you folks didn't decide on this Project on my account," were the first words out of the Foxie's mouth.

"We realize it is a big Project," JJ conceded.

"Big!" Foxie exclaimed, "Do you expect anyone to survive this Project?" He inquired.

"That's the reason we always give the final say to the Team on all projects," Mac informed Foxie, "If they say no, we move on to another project."

"I was hoping you would say something like that," a relieved Foxie replied, "Well nothing is impossible. I'll start kicking it around in my head and if the Team gives it a go, I'll contribute all I can."

"Fair enough," JJ acknowledged, then continued with alternate projects if the Team passed on this one.

CHAPTER TWO

One week had passed since the presentation and the Team had been meeting every day to study the project. The who and what had been answered by the project itself. The where, when, and especially HOW, had been the topics of discussion.

JJ and Mac were attending the Team meeting that morning to get their decision and would understand if the Team decided to pass on this one.

Everyone was already seated when JC walked to the front of the room and called the meeting to order.

"Morning, sports fans," JC greeted everyone in attendance.

"Morning," was the group's reply.

"As you all know we are here to inform JJ and Mac of our decision on the proposed Project," JC started, "First, we all feel this Project is too large for a team of ten with little or no backup from a bigger organization. If it was a Team of ten with CIA resources backing them up, it would be another story."

"Second, the planning and training would take months. To date we have taken on smaller Projects where planning, training and the project itself were completed in a month or two."

"I could go on," JC conceded as he looked at JJ and Mac, "but I guess our answer is a tentative yes."

JJ's thought process was already preparing a reply of *'The Board and myself totally understand your turning down this project,'* when the process was interrupted with the words "tentative yes."

JJ gave Mac a questioning look and Mac responded with, "You heard him right, I'm surprised too."

JJ looked back at JC and inquired, "Are you all sure about this?"

"Yes," JC replied, "But it's a tentative yes. We all feel the timing of this project is just ahead of the curve for a major

disaster, but also feel you and the Board have no idea about the amount of financing of a project like this."

"I think we do," JJ quickly replied, "One of our Board members used to dabble in that area years ago." JJ was of course referring to Gil Dunn, former DDO at CIA. As Deputy Director of Operations, Gil had to give the okay on similar projects and knew exactly what was involved in the planning and financing.

"Then with your approval we will start detailed planning and other preparations," JC announced.

"You have it," JJ answered, "but the Board, including Mac and myself, want to make something perfectly clear. If you hit a problem during the planning you feel is too big, let us know and the project will be canceled. We are very serious about this. We'll just move on to another project with no additional discussion."

JC and the Team acknowledged JJ's words and would comply with the Board's wishes, for the most part anyway.

JC took back control of the meeting and announced, "Since the Project is a go, we have a few issues we should cover ASAP."

JC addressed JJ. "First is communications. This is extremely important," JC reaffirmed, "We will require state of the art equipment that will reach anywhere in the world if necessary."

"Second, in the original planning from the Board a device was mentioned. How will we get something that sophisticated?" JC questioned.

"The Board will take care of that item," JJ assured, "One of our members is already involved in high level planning on how to acquire it."

"Let me guess who that is," Blue Jay whispered to Bean who smiled and shook his head in agreement.

With item number two satisfied, JC moved on. "Third, we will require three fifty-caliber rifles with the latest day-night imaging type scopes, silencers, the works."

JJ looked at Mac and inquired, "Maybe I can get Charley Tuna to sell us back those two fifties the Team gave him during the Cuba Project."

"Maybe," Mac replied, "but I doubt it. Tuna probably already sold them to a chop shop. They've probably been broken up and sold as parts."

"Why don't I believe there is a big demand for fifty-caliber rifle parts in Cuba?" JJ inquired.

"Because you're a non-believer?" Mac took a guess.

JC saw where this conversation was headed and interrupted it with additional requirements.

"Sorry JJ, we will require more firepower on this one. The two used for the Cuba Project were bolt action. We require Semi automatic fifties this time."

JJ acknowledged JC's request, as he made an entry in his notebook. JJ would get anything the Team wanted or needed, but he and Mac had an on-going thing about what really happened to the two rifles used in Cuba.

With those items taken care of, JC addressed the room. "Does anyone have any other questions or concerns at this time? No one," he confirmed, "Then I guess it's time for a coffee break. Top and the Ladies have prepared something for us at the house."

That said everyone stood, left the team meeting room, and headed for the house.

JJ noticed the Team was unusually quiet as they moved toward the house. *'Were they having second thoughts or were they already thinking about the detailed planning stage of the Project?'*

That question was answered after the Team was seated around the special extra-large dining room table JJ purchased so the Team, House Staff, Mac, and himself could be seated at the same time.

"Well, here we are again," Air Jockey announced, "So Top, have you been watching Emeril on the food channel to get some new ideas for meals or will we be getting the usual souped up World War II C-Rations again?"

"I'll give you C-Rations, you little pecker head," Top fired back.

The entire Team burst into laughter and knew that was the opening shot of what they had come to know as The Bull Shit Derby. This was the first time they had all been seated together since their return, so this Derby would probably go on for hours and cover many subjects.

'Well that answers the, are they having second thoughts question,' JJ thought, *'This is SOP for the Team. In deep thought when planning a Project and raising hell the rest of the time.'*

RON WOOTTERS

Project planning and training were proceeding at the Barn. Check was holding language classes each morning for the entire Team, then they all broke into small groups.

Check, Tick, and Bris were planning the best escape routes including several alternatives.

Blue Jay would be joining Pru and Met on the .50 caliber rifles along with their spotters Bean, Benz, and Panda, who were still in the planning and dry fire stages.

Air Jockey would be operating one of those technical gizmos and with JC's help was getting proficient in its use.

The Teams days were dedicated to the Project in addition to their usual physical fitness activities. After dinner, in the evening, and weekends were still left open to do what they liked.

The Project was on.

CHAPTER THREE

Gil Dunn was hard at work trying to close an arms deal when his private line rang. Getting a little disturbed for being interrupted he answered the phone with a brisk, "Hello!"

"Are you in the middle of something?" the voice on the phone inquired.

"No, not at all," answered Gil after he realized the voice belonged to Di Flipi, a co-worker from his CIA days.

"Haven't heard from you since that post 911 episode. How are things going?"

"Funny you should mention that," Di Flipi replied, "I have another situation that is pretty much the same thing."

"Let's hear it," Gil offered.

"I'm afraid we would have to meet for me to explain this one," Di Flipi explained.

"Okay," Gil replied slowly, "how do you want to work this?"

"I can take a train to Penn Station in New York City tomorrow and meet you somewhere in the city."

"That would be good," Gil said as he wondered what the rush was and why he couldn't tell him over the phone. It was either something hot or Di Flipi had sniffed out what he was into. Either way they had to meet.

"Let's see, today is Thursday, why don't you plan to come up tomorrow and stay for the weekend at my place?"

"I don't want to impose," Di Flipi answered.

"Nonsense," Dunn exclaimed, "My family is all off somewhere, so I'm on my own this weekend. It will give us a chance to catch up."

"Sounds good," Di Flipi agreed, "I'll catch a train that puts me into the city around noon. Since I'll be in the Big Apple, I should go visit John's widow to pay my respects. Grand old gal and as diplomatic as a runaway train," Di Flipi laughed.

"That she is," Dunn agreed, "Well, give me a call when you finish your visit."

15

"Okay," Di Flipi confirmed, "see you then."

As Gil hung up the phone he thought to himself, *'It has been a while since I had to do this, now let me see. John's widow are the alert words and the following sentence tells me the location. Grand old gal and as diplomatic as a runaway train. First and last words Grand and Train. Grand and Train in New York City. He's coming into Penn Station, but wants me to pick him up at Grand Central Train Station. This is starting to sound serious and with running this company, being a member of the Board with JJ and Company, I already have a full plate and don't need any unnecessary trouble.*

Ah, what the fuck, at least I know I'm still alive.' Gil dismissed his concerns as he returned his attention back to the arm's deal.

The following day Gil Dunn was circling Grand Central Station and wondering if he had the correct location. As he slowly drove down the left side of the building for the third time, he saw a man walk to the curb that resembled Di Flipi. The man gave a small wave with his right hand and Dunn brought his car to a stop. Seconds later Di Flipi was in the car and Gil pulled away.

"Long time no see, spy man," Dunn quipped.

"It has been a long time," agreed Di Flipi, "almost eight years."

"You're lucky I remembered the procedure correctly," Dunn remarked, "I could be circling the MGM Grand in Vegas right now."

"Sorry about that," Di Flipi said, "have something hot. Is there a secure place we can talk?"

"I think that can be arranged," Gil agreed then changed the subject to catching up on family and old friends.

It was mid-afternoon when Dunn pulled into his driveway and the garage doors started to open. By the time the Lincoln reached the doors they were open and Gil pulled right in, hit a button and the doors started to close again.

"Nice house," an impressed Di Flipi exclaimed.

"The result of a capitalist society," Dunn announced.

"Amen to that," replied Di Flipi.

As both men got out of the car, Gil grabbed the overnight bag in the backseat, but Di Flipi kept control of the PC case.

As they entered the house Gil inquired, "Ready for a brew?"

"Sounds good," replied Di Flipi.

Dunn put the bag down in the hallway then led his old partner to his den. After dealing with a few locks Gil opened the door, ushered Di Flipi in then inquired, "What are you drinking these days?"

"Vodka is good," replied Di Flipi.

Dunn poured two vodka and club sodas, offered one to his friend, and gestured toward two chairs. When both men were seated, Dunn started the conversation. "I must admit you have my curiosity stirred up. Is this another case like the 911 aftermath where the Agency wouldn't listen to you and you were right?"

"No, not at all," Di answered, "This time everything was working out well. The situation was in a foreign country and I was the control. Since that 911 aftermath situation, where mysterious forces came in to save the day," Di Flipi announced, as he nodded toward Gil, "I have been running a section in the new Counter Terrorist Group."

Gil was wondering how his look of wonderment was holding up since Di made that statement about "mysterious forces."

"Before I get any deeper into this, I'll give you the bottom line," Di Flipi suggested. "The situation has moved to U.S. soil and you know what that means. More and more people will know until it winds up in the media, the bad people change their mode of operation, and we are left sucking hind tit again."

"What are you suggesting, Di?" inquired Gil.

"I need someone to get a piece of information without screwing up and blowing the entire operation," Di said as he took a sip from his drink then looked at Gil. "Do you remember those two kids, Blue Jay and Bean, that worked for you at the Agency back in the mid-nineties?"

"How could I forget?" Gil replied, "I think they ran me through every emotion there is. I went from threatening them with prison, to liking them and being their strongest supporter, sometimes all in the same week."

"I remember," Di said as he dropped his head in laughter, "Do you know how I could get in touch with them?" Di Flipi asked.

"I could make inquiries," Gil offered, "but I would have to know what the situation is."

"Fair enough," Di replied, "Is this room secure?"

"Yes," was the one-word reply.

"You're not going to believe this one," started Di. "Last year we discovered one of the ways Al-Qaida is now communicating to their agents around the world. Since that reporter told everyone how NSA could listen in on Bin Laden's cell phone conversations, they have been looking into ways of how they could to use low tech."

"How did you manage to penetrate Al-Qaida and get that type of information?" Dunn inquired.

"We didn't," Di Flipi answered. "We don't even know the identity of the source. We got a note in the mail and after telling us what dogs we are, the person or persons stated their objections to the methods being used, then explained how it was being done. We checked it out and after a little code breaking discovered we had a genuine source. We have been getting the info for evaluation at the same time their agents are, but now the operation has moved to the U.S. and we need additional information to continue being effective."

"And that's why you want Blue Jay and Bean," Dunn replied, "Blue Jay can get in and out of anywhere while Bean covers him."

"That's about it," Di Flipi agreed.

"Is that it?" Dunn fired back. "I think you have been working with those new breed of Agency dicks too long. You want me to find two former agents, get them involved in something that could get them in trouble with the law or killed by Al-Qaida and, wait a minute, let's not forget how you're telling me about all of this. What is it called, the dysentery method, give out the facts in dribbles?"

"If you feel that way I can always find and recruit them

myself," Di Flipi snapped.

"Not if I find them first," Dunn assured Di Flipi, "You're not getting my people fucked up, let the Fed's get what you want."

"What do you mean, 'my people?'" Di Flipi inquired.

"What?" replied Dunn, knowing he misspoke and that Di picked up on it.

"You said, 'You're not getting my people fucked up,' Di Flipi asked again.

"Well, they were my people at the Agency," Dunn tried to explain.

"That was ten years ago and old news. Your statement was talking about the present," Di accused.

Gil knew he screwed up and started a barrage of bull to cover his mistake, but Di Flipi interrupted his barrage with, "I think you have been working with those new breed of Corporate dicks too long. You fell right into that one."

"Let's see, what are the ingredients, one part giving out info very slowly, one part asking for assistance, one part telling him you don't need his assistance and boom, pissed-off man slips up."

While Di was enjoying himself Dunn was thinking, *Okay he got me. That pecker head is still good or am I slipping? Well, I guess it's on to plan B, whatever that is? Maybe Di will help me?'*

"You seem to be very sure of yourself," Gil said to Di Flipi.

"Yes I am," Di replied, "and it's not just the slip. I have picked up on other things."

"Like what?" Dunn inquired.

"Like catching glimpses of Blue Jay on security cameras around Washington last year during that terrorist with a nuclear suitcase episode. Blue Jay is very good, but there are just so many cameras around the city it is impossible to dodge them all."

"So the Agency knows about this?" Dunn inquired.

"Are you kidding?" Di exploded, "I know it because I know Blue Jay and that's as far as it has to go."

"If that's the case guess I should level with you," Dunn confessed, "After I left the Agency I started missing the action. You know going from DDO to the business world is a big drop in excitement. Anyway, about five years ago I decided to create a two-man team for small stuff and of course Blue Jay and Bean

19

came to mind. When I hear about things and feel they are important enough, like your call about the terrorist theory, I get them involved."

'I wonder if he is buying this?' Dunn wondered, and also wonders, *'what Di would do if he knew about the Team, the Board, and how they were all involved in the Washington, terrorist, and Nuc suitcase episode?'*

When Gil was done with his briefing he looked to Di Flipi for feedback.

"That's a good story, if it's true," Di announced, "but that doesn't really matter. I just need someone to get information for me."

"If it doesn't matter, why did you push the buttons?" Dunn inquired.

"Just curious," was the simple reply.

"I never liked you when you worked for me at the Agency," Dunn informed Di.

"Not at all?" Di Flipi inquired as he burst into laughter.

"Not at all. Give me your glass," instructed Gil as he stood, "we need a refill."

After taking a few sips of their fresh drinks and remembering other humorous situations from the past, the mood changed back to a more serious note when Di Flipi returned to the original topic.

"Since my curiosity is satisfied, let me give you the whole story about how Al-Qaida is sending communications to their agents around the world," Di Flipi announced as he went to retrieve his PC bag.

When he returned he removed the PC from the bag and placed it on Gil's desk.

"Need an outlet?" Gil asked.

"No, I have a fresh battery in it," answered Di, as he once again went into the bag, removed a large magnifying glass and a mirror, then placed the bag on the floor.

"Now at this point an Al-Qaida agent anywhere in the world just needs to turn on a PC, dial into the Internet, and go to a certain site to get their info," Di Flipi informed Gil. "We are not going to do that. I will explain how they are doing it and I have a copy of what they are after on this," he remarked as he removed a diskette from his shirt pocket.

"I thought the Intel Community were watching suspected web sites?" Dunn asked.

"We are and know they are using certain sites. The problem is they know we are aware of certain sites, so who knows what they are really using them for now?"

"They generate a lot of traffic on those sites and the U.S. starts sounding bells and blowing whistles."

"I've noticed that," Gil agreed.

"Anyway, here is how our little part of the counter terrorist pie works," Di Flipi continued. "First, we all know these terrorists are nuts, but they are not stupid. Anyone that doesn't believe that just has to look at the first time they went after the World Trade Center. They came damn close to accomplishing their total plan of a domino effect where the tower would fall into the other tower then both would crash onto Wall Street and all of the people there."

Gil shook his head in agreement and Di continued.

"As I said earlier, after Bin Laden got wind about NSA and his cell phone conversations, they started looking low tech and my guess is their analysis went something like this.

One, do not have a network of their own and if they did U.S. Intel would sniff it out. Two, ease of use for Al-Qaida agents.

Three, make net-work as large as possible. Four, make it difficult to detect. See where I am going with this?" Di Inquired.

"The Internet, right?" Gil answered.

"The Internet with a twist," added Di, "They found everything they needed in the porn industry. A network that already existed, is easy to use and you just sign on to the Internet. It is worldwide with thousands of sites making it easy to hide and move around in, while using very low-tech communication to send messages and instructions to their agents. All this, plus my personal favorite," Di added, "Remember Al-Qaida in Afghanistan and how the women had to wear burkas? Now what is the exact opposite of that and a place where Intel may not even look? Talk about Hijacking a religion and using it for your own benefit."

"That's clever, but how do they send messages?" Gil inquired.

"Well, the participants must look American and may or may not be aware of the message sending. I'll show you why," Di said as he put the floppy diskette into the PC, then clicked on media player. A few more clicks and the screen was filled with a man and woman having sex in a bedroom.

"Well this is interesting," remarked Dunn, "What's he doing, pumping the message out in Morse code?"

"Patience," replied Di as he moved the PC cursor to a position over stop.

After a brief stay watching the couple, the camera panned around the room until it got to a large dresser with a mirror. When it picked up the mirror reflection of the couple on the bed, it stopped and once again the couple were the main event.

At this point, Di Flipi clicked the mouse on the PC and the picture froze. He then placed the mirror opposite the PC screen and picked up the magnifying glass.

Di saw that he had Gil's total attention and handed him the magnifying glass. "Want to see if you still have any of that DDO shit still working?"

Gil smiled and answered, "Yeah," as he accepted the glass and started scanning the screen.

He started at the lower left corner and slowly moved to the right until he reached the lower right corner, then he moved the magnifying glass up about a half inch, then moved back to the left. Dunn repeated this process until he detected a piece of writing paper on the dresser.

"I see writing paper on the dresser," he informed Di Flipi.

"And?" Di inquired.

"It looks like it's folded in half with the bottom laying flat on the dresser and the top half sticking up in the air, but nothing seems to be written on it," Gil said slowly.

"Are you looking at the paper now? Di asked.

"Yes," Gil confirmed.

"Then come straight up very slowly from that position."

Gil started moving the glass as instructed and in a matter of seconds discovered he could see the other side of the sheet of paper and the writing on it in the reflection of the mirror.

"That's clever," Dunn announced, "but the writing is upside down and backward."

"That's to discourage anyone that may have discovered it,"

Di Flipi added, "They would just assume it was a letter left on the dresser and return to all of the other action going on in the reflection, but if someone did take the time, the message is also encoded."

"For all us folks, good and bad, that know what we are looking for, we employ a second mirror," Di Flipi informed Gil, as he positioned the mirror he had removed from his bag closer to the screen. After a little adjustment he instructed Gil to approach the mirror from the back and look over the top until he could see the reflection of the letter in the mirror.

Dunn followed the instructions then announced, "The message is right side up and reads from left to right."

"Just a little convenience for decoding purposes," Di informed Gil.

"Have you turned up any good Intel?" Dunn inquired.

"Let's say we have intercepted a few people that were sent out to do bad things and we did bad things to them first," Di Flipi answered.

"It works for me," approved Dunn.

"That brings you up-to-date on their low-tech communication system and how we are monitoring it," Di Flipi informed Gil, "Now I'll tell you why we need Blue Jay and Bean. For security reasons, Al-Qaida moves these message movies and others like it around the Internet. To accomplish this they supply each operative with a key that gives them the new website and date the movie will be shown. Without that you could be searching the web forever looking for it. When their operation was overseas, we had the resources to get the new key listings, but since they moved their operations to the U.S., it's a different story. If we do find it and something happens or if the media gets a hold of it, we could lose it all."

"Understood," Gil assured Di Flipi. "I'll get in touch with Blue Jay and Bean. Do you want to be in on the meeting?"

"Yes," Di said with an upbeat reply. "I would like to see those kids again."

"Okay," Gil agreed as he thought to himself, 'decision time. Do I call this one on my own or bring the Board in on it?'

CHAPTER FOUR

Due to the importance and sensitive nature of this project, Dunn had decided to make the call himself. He was sure under normal circumstances the Board would agree, but since the planning of the largest project to date was underway someone may have second thoughts.

Gil would have no problem if Blue Jay and Bean's decision was to pass on Di's situation.

Dunn was in touch with Blue Jay, via cell phone, Friday night and suggested they all get together with their mutual friend before he returned to his home in Utah.

Blue Jay required no additional information. He didn't know who the mutual friend was, but knew something had to be very important for Dunn to break all the rules set up by the Board.

Thinking quickly Blue Jay decides on a location.

"Are you familiar with Stover Park just outside of Point Pleasant, Pennsylvania?" Blue Jay inquired.

"No, but I'll find it," Gil reassured him.

"When you arrive, follow the signs for The High Rocks."

"Tell John to bring his camera, we'll bring the beer," Blue Jay added.

"Sounds good," Dunn said, "see you around 2." and hung up.

Saturday morning Bean and Blue Jay were driving north on Route 32 towards Point Pleasant, Pennsylvania. The meeting wasn't until 2 P.M., but the duo didn't want any surprises.

Blue Jay and Bean were wondering why Dunn requested this meeting, but were prepared for anything, even the very unlikely prospect of a setup. Both were in agreement on this point, but it was better to be sure than be sorry. They would lay low and check out the area for hours prior to Dunn's arrival.

At 1:30 P.M. Dunn and Di Flipi were driving south on Route 32 just outside of Point Pleasant, Pennsylvania. Five minutes later they were entering the very small burg and located the road to Stover Park. Another ten minutes and they were in the park and had located the High Rocks parking area. After parking the Lincoln, and with the PC case in tow, the two followed a path that ran along the top of the cliffs. They didn't know where Blue Jay and Bean were, but were sure they would show up sooner or later.

People used the high rocks to practice rock climbing, rappelling, and certain areas were marked for those purposes. The two passed A drop, B drop, and were approaching C drop when a voice from behind them asked, "Is that you Di Flipi?"

Both men on the path knew that voice belonged to Bean.

"Yeah, it's me," Di Flipi confirmed.

"Well, how the hell are you," a voice rang out not two feet from where Dunn and Di Flipi were standing causing them both to jump back a little.

"These kids haven't changed a bit," Di Flipi observed.

"Tell me about it," Gil agreed, "they almost gave me a heart attack."

"Sorry about that," Blue Jay apologized.

"Maybe the picnic we setup on top of C drop will make amends," Bean offered.

"Any beer?" Gil inquires.

"Of course, but if you see a Park Ranger, deep six it into the basket," Blue Jay warned.

"Fair enough," Dunn agreed, "lead on."

The four men spent the first hour or so remembering old times, old friends, and enjoying the food.

After taking the last sip of his beer Dunn changed the topic to the subject at hand. "I'm sure you're wondering why Di and myself requested this meeting." Gil started.

"It had crossed our minds," Bean answered.

"Well here's the scoop. Di came to me to discuss a situation that needed immediate attention. I told him how the three of us have been taking on small projects for the past five years. He will brief you," Dunn continued, "and if you think it is doable and will not cause any unforeseen problems, we'll start planning."

Bean and Blue Jay took their cue from that statement. Di Flipi didn't know about the Board or the Team and the other members of the Board probably weren't aware of Di Flipi and his situation. For now Dunn wanted to keep it that way.

While Dunn was talking, Di Flipi took the PC, mirror, and magnifying glass out of the PC bag.

When Gil finished talking he gestured toward Di Flipi and he started the briefing while Gil kept the area under surveillance for any climbers, hikers, or anyone else that might be passing through.

When Di finished the briefing he inquired, "Any thoughts or comments?"

"Well, they certainly found a low tech way to communicate and are using a network that already exists," offered Blue Jay.

"And how they are using the web goes way out of bounds for the Muslim faith and would probably be dismissed in the Intel community," added Bean.

"That's true," Di agreed, "but one thing they didn't count on was someone from inside their own organization getting disgusted by the method and dropping us a line about it."

"Really?" Bean asks.

"Yes," answered Di. "Our guess is the person wants to bring the method to a halt and figured if we found out about it, we would shut it down, and Al-Qaida would move on to some other way to communicate."

"Have you gotten anything good out of monitoring them?" Blue Jay asked.

"Yes," Di confirmed, "and I'll give you an example of why a copy of the key is so important. Using the key, we were monitoring the site and got a new message. By the time we got it decoded, things turned into a race and we didn't even have time to notify the Feds."

"So it happened in the U.S.?" Bean asked.

"There was a thing on the news a few months ago about a man being found dead at a New York airport, but their wasn't any follow-up on it," Di offered.

"I remember that," Blue Jay replied. "Wondered why the media dropped it?"

"Well, an operative got instructions to shoot his way past security and blow himself up, but we got lucky."

"One of our people spotted a suspicious looking man in a stairwell and pressured him a little. The man panicked and attempted to pull a weapon, but our man was faster."

"Without the key we have to search for the website and that would be very time consuming. In the case I just told you about, the outcome would have been very different."

"You say they moved the operation to the U.S.?" Blue Jay inquired.

"That is correct," Di confirmed.

"Why don't you just intercept one of the agents and take the key?"

"Two reasons," Di replied, "We don't know who the agents are until we have to intercept them and then if it's in a crowd its hide-and-seek, but the main reason is each agent does not have a complete key. The man that runs the operation is the only one that has a copy of the master key and with that we can monitor all transmissions. Problem is he keeps it in his possession at all times."

"So Bean, how are we going to get a copy of the list?" inquired Blue Jay.

"Simple," Bean quickly replied, "Figure I'll walk up to him and tell him his shoelace is untied and when he looks I'll hit him with a sapper. While he's out cold, I'll take pictures of the key list."

"Sounds like a plan to me," approved Blue Jay.

Di Flipi just smiled and shook his head. "Gil, remember how these two used to drive people at the Agency up the wall when asked how they were going to do something?"

"They deserved it," Bean responded, "They would explain a problem, and then expect us to have a plan to fix it at a second's notice."

"And some were very slow on the uptake," added Blue Jay, "What was the name of that one boss we had, was it Gun or Fun?"

"Dunn," Bean offered.

"That's right, Dunn," Blue Jay acknowledged, "He always did that."

"I just wanted to hear the joke of the day," Gil defended.

As everyone broke into laughter, Di Flipi exclaimed, "I see things haven't changed much."

"Did you really think they would?" asked Dunn.

"This is just a wild guess, Dunn continued, "but does that mean it's a go for this one?"

Both men shook their heads in agreement.

"Do we have a location and a picture of this turd?" Blue Jay inquired.

"Yes," Di answered as he once again went into his PC bag and produced an envelope.

After taking a break while a scout troop hiked passed, Di Flipi continued the briefing, this time focusing on the subject, his location and a sample of what the key list looked like the last time the Agency managed to get a copy of it in Europe.

Briefing completed, Blue Jay and Bean promised they would kick it around and come up with a plan by the following day. At that point the four again relaxed, enjoyed the conversation and the beautiful view from C drop.

The following morning Blue Jay and Bean were in the process of presenting their idea to Di Flipi and Dunn.

"Since this turd probably has the only master key list, he probably keeps it very close at all times. It will be very hairy, but here is our idea. We will do it in two phases," Blue Jay started, "First, when the apartment is empty, I will put in listening and video devices. After a check, we will put them into quiet mode and not activate them again until we prepare for entry."

"Hopefully, the following day," Bean continued, "when he is indisposed, Blue Jay will make entry, get a picture of the key, retrieve the video and listening devices, and then depart."

"This is too hairy," Dunn disapproved, "what is plan B?"

Without hesitation Blue Jay replied, "Bean and his sapper."

"I still say that is the way to go," Bean offered as he

demonstrated his sapper swing.

Dunn looked at Bean then at Blue Jay and asked, "So how long do you think it will take you to get in and out with the stuff."

"As fast as I can," Blue Jay announced.

"That brings up another item," Bean added as he looked at Dunn, "we could use another pair of hands on this one."

"How so?" inquired Gil.

"If I'm covering his back outside," Bean started his reply,

"I wouldn't be able to monitor the video, audio, communicate to Blue Jay when to move, and the status of the turd."

"So you want me to monitor the gear and communications, is that it?" Gil asked.

"You'll like it," Blue Jay informed Gil, "It will be like the old days. We located a radio tower in the neighborhood and from the top of it you should have a clear view of the area."

"It's not as bad as it sounds," Bean added, "The climb to the top may be rough, but if all goes well you'll have a nice parachute ride down. However if things don't go well, you'll only have one round so don't miss."

"Don't miss!" Di Flipi exploded, "we can't kill this guy. If we do we will lose all connections."

"The rounds not for the turd, it's for him," Blue Jay corrected as he pointed to Dunn. "If anything goes, wrong the first thing he should do is shoot himself."

"You will be carrying a rifle so don't forget to wear those split-toed sneakers you bought in Korea," Bean instructed, "It will make it easier for you to get your big toe on the trigger."

Bean and Blue Jay looked at each other and burst into laughter.

"Enjoy yourself," Dunn informed the duo, "because every dog has its day."

Di Flipi wanted to laugh, but didn't want to make Dunn mad, so he quickly asked a question instead.

"I know you're not serious about the tower, but where will Gil be monitoring from?"

"Well, let's think about that," Blue Jay pondered as he looked at Di Flipi. "Your people have the turd under surveillance, right?"

"Yes," confirmed Di, "an apartment across the street."

"Why don't you call off surveillance the nights we will be running the operation so Uncle Fudd can use the apartment for monitoring?"

"Every dog has it's day," Dunn again informed the duo.

A few more details were discussed and the operation was put on hold until the following week.

———————

It was Monday evening and a dark blue Z28 had just parked at the curb in front of the Bucks County Fencing Academy in Lambertville, New Jersey. Blue Jay and Bean fenced at the Barn with the other Team members and once a week tried to fence at this club.

Due to the conversations that went on between the two when they were fencing, Mark, the Fencing Master and owner, requested they fence with each other prior to virgin ears coming into the building.

As the duo approached one of the fencing strips to begin their saber match, that usually generated the most conversation, Bean inquired, "I wonder what will happen if the boss finds out about this new deal?"

"Don't know," Blue Jay replied, "are you worried about it?"

"No," Bean answered, "just wondering."

"Well, wonder over there, Nancy Marie," Blue Jay said as he used his saber and pointed to a position opposite him on the strip.

"Nancy Marie is it?" Bean fired back as he moved to the position.

There was more conversation than usual during their fencing this evening that, for some unknown reason, caused a woman visiting the club for the first time to run into the Fencing Master's office claiming two men were about to get into a fight in the fencing area.

The remainder of the week Blue Jay and Bean used the evenings to check out the area around their next operation, while at the same time staying out of the sight of the surveillance Di Flipi had on going.

———————

The following Friday night had arrived and after satisfying themselves that the turd would be out for a while, the three were in position. The first night Dunn would monitor the area and alert Blue Jay and Bean of any and all undesirables in the area.

Bean would be to the left and Blue Jay would stay close to the building's brick wall and move slowly toward the patio door of the end unit.

"Are you on, Bean?" Blue Jay asked, as he spoke quietly into his com unit.

"I'm on," is a soft reply.

"Are you on, One Round," Blue Jay asked checking in with the third man on the team.

"Every dog has its day," was the reply.

Blue Jay had a big smile on his face as he checked the area one last time then announced, "Let's do it."

Di Flipi warned them this was not the best part of town, that dead bodies could be discovered at any given time and he wasn't kidding.

In addition to watching out for terrorists they had armed street scum to worry about that would sooner shoot you and take your valuables than say, this is a stick up.

Blue Jay was moving slowly toward the patio with Bean about twenty yards to his left and a little back. The two men stopped from time to time due to unexpected noise or when instructed by Dunn.

"This place reminds me of Lebanon," Bean whispered into the com.

"Tell me about it."

The two were halfway to the door when Dunn came on the com with an excited voice. "Just saw a shadow on the wall very close behind Blue Jay."

Blue Jay went into a crouch position as he turned and pointed his weapon in that direction.

At the same time Bean turned to his right swinging his weapon back and forth behind Blue Jay's position looking for any sign of movement.

After a slight pause Dunn's voice came over the com. "Sorry

about that, it must have been Lamont Cranston passing through."

"Would this fall into the category of, Every dog has its day?" Inquired Bean.

"RUFF!" and a little chuckle were the only replies.

"Touché," Blue Jay said as he and Bean turned and headed for their destination.

Once Blue Jay reached the patio door he quickly picked the lock and was inside the apartment as Bean took up a position next to a hedge that is directly across from the patio.

Blue Jay turned on his flashlight, put it in his mouth, and secured it with his teeth. Nothing fancy for the devices, just a place they would not be discovered for a day or so, listening and video devices under the night stand in the bedroom.

That done Blue Jay requested, "Activation and test," over the com unit.

"Activated," Dunn replied.

"Audio test," Blue Jay said softly at a distance.

"Audio okay," Gil replied into the com.

Blue Jay then moved a few move feet away from the night stand knelt down, and shined the flashlight directly at his hand.

"Video test," Blue Jay informed Dunn

"Video okay, Gil replied.

With both tests completed, Dunn shut down both devices until they were needed again.

Blue Jay made a quick survey of the apartment before leaving. One bedroom, one bath, very small kitchen, and one big room part living room, part dining area. Windows were half-sliding, but big enough to make an exit if needed, and one door to the hallway. Blue Jay walked over to the hallway door and looked through the peephole, and then checked around the door for any security devices. The usual lock in the door knob, two dead bolts, one can be operated with a key, one strictly for in side security, and a security chain. The balcony door had the same setup with the addition of a cheap device that sounded off if it is turned on and the door is opened. Since this turd liked to keep a low profile on his comings and goings, he used the patio door so the internal locks and the alarm device didn't come into play this time, but Blue Jay had to quickly find another way to enter on his next visit. *'In order to get in and out while someone was in the apartment, the windows were probably the only option.'* He thought to himself as he started checking the windows facing the patio. A picture window, a door, and another picture window. Nothing there. Continuing his scan from side-to-side Blue Jay discovered small sliding windows at the bottom of each picture window and immediately investigated. No additional security, just the basic lock that came with the window. *'Here is my entry point,'* Blue Jay thought as he removed a small packet of tools and set to the task of altering the window lock so it would still seem to be locked if checked, but if forced a little would open. Halfway through his modification Blue Jay received an inquiry from Bean,

"You on?"

"Yeah, I'm on," Blue Jay answered.

"Are you watching one of his movies in there?" Bean inquired.

"Yeah," Blue Jay replied, "and the star is wearing a green hat. It's called, Conquests of the Green Bo-dean."

"Is that what it's called?" Bean replied quickly. "Well if you don't get a move on, the next one will be called, Look What I Found in My Apartment."

"I'm almost done, making exit in a few seconds," Blue Jay informed Bean.

Twenty seconds later Blue Jay was asking for permission to exit the building. Bean made one last scan of the area and gave the okay. Blue Jay quickly exited the apartment and locked the door. The two then took a different route out of the area and walked for blocks in order to detect any tail they might have picked up. That completed, they rejoined Dunn at the surveillance apartment.

"Well, phase one went smoothly," Dunn said confidently.

"So far," offered Blue Jay. "I wonder what other type of surveillance gear they have here."

"Why?" Dunn inquired.

"I had to modify the lock on one of the windows and would like to make sure no one discovers it."

"Let's take a look in those cases," Dunn suggested as he

pointed to three cases against the wall.

"This laser gear will work," Blue Jay announced as he displayed the contents of one of the cases. "If we aim for the upper right hand corner of the picture window we should pick up anyone checking the locked window or discovering the lock isn't working properly."

"That will work," Bean approved as he moved a table over to a window facing the patio window across the street.

The three men almost had the laser set up, but can't get the proper angle for the laser beam.

Dunn was routing through the other cases on the floor when he said, "Duct tape; this shit will fix anything!"

After a few minutes of zeroing in the beam and a shit load of duct tape, the device was turned on. From now on any noise around the window would be transmitted to the surveillance apartment.

That completed, the three set up who would stand what shifts during the night and then decided to get some rest.

CHAPTER FIVE

Not much activity happened during the next day. The Turd departed at mid-morning. Now night was starting to arrive and he hadn't returned. The trio saw this as a good thing; hopefully it would eliminate the need for a day entry. Bean and Blue Jay had their Gas Company uniforms on, but a night entry would be much better.

It was 10:20 P.M. when the Turd finally returned to his apartment. Upon his arrival, Blue Jay and Bean immediately left and took up positions close to the Turds apartment. Dunn had activated all systems and was keeping the duo informed about the subject's activities. When he turned on the bathroom light, the interest level picked up. Bean and Blue Jay moved in a little closer and waited. The subject started to unbutton his shirt as he reached for the hot water faucet in the shower.

"This may be it," Dunn informed the other two, as he kept his eyes glued to the video monitor.

The subject returned to the bedroom, continued to undress, and then returned to the bathroom wearing only a pair of shorts, and closed the door.

When Dunn relayed that, Blue Jay instructed, "Let's do it," and he and Bean moved quickly to the patio.

Blue Jay removed the screen on the window he had prepared for entry, applied a small suction cup to the window, gave a quick yank, and the window was unlocked.

That completed, he alerted Dunn. "Ready."

"Do it," was the reply from Gil.

Blue Jay quickly but quietly slid the window open and crawled into the apartment. All of the lights were on so if he was discovered now, he was just a person wearing a Gas man's uniform trying to explain how he got into the apartment. More likely Al-Qaida will be missing a movie maker.

Blue Jay moved to the bedroom looking for any thing that could contain the key list when he spotted a large billfold on the bed. Opening it he saw money and after additional searching discovered a folded piece of paper stuck in the back compartment. Blue Jay removed, unfolded it, discovered very small print, and what looked like a year's worth of schedules.

Blue Jay spread the paper out on the bed, removed a small camera from his pocket, focused in on the paper, and pressed the shutter button. He let six or seven shots roll by before letting up on the button. After going through all of this shit, a bad picture just wouldn't do. That completed, he replaced the camera into his pocket then refolded the paper and placed it back into the wallet making sure it was exactly the way he found it.

After closing the billfold, Blue Jay started to retrieve the audio and video devices when he heard the toilet flush in the bathroom. Not sure what the subject would do next he moved out of the line of sight to the bathroom and to the other side of the bed. A few seconds later he heard a noise from the knob on the bathroom door, quickly laid down beside the bed, and tried to get under it, but it was too low. With his left arm and leg squeezed under the bed and the remainder of his body hugging it, Blue Jay waited with gun in hand.

The subject left the bath and entered the bedroom. "Playing hide-and-seek with me, AH!" the subject announced as he moved toward the bed.

From his position Blue Jay could only see the subject's feet from under the bed and was not sure if he had a weapon. *'Well he was talking to somebody so I'll give him two more steps in this direction, then he's history!'*

'One, two,' Blue Jay counted and was in the process of rising up when the subject stopped, turned and walked away from the bed.

"He was after the billfold," a relieved Dunn informed Blue Jay. "He went back into the bathroom."

Blue Jay held his position until it sounded like a shower was in process. He then stood, recovered the devices, and made for the window.

"Ready to exit," Blue Jay announced.

"Do it," Bean answered without hesitation.

Once outside, he used the suction cup to close and lock the window. He then removed the suction cup and cleaned the window to remove any telltale circle the cup may have left behind. After replacing the screen he and Bean departed the area using separate routes.

Dunn would continue general surveillance of the area until Blue Jay and Bean returned. He kept them in view as they made their way back. All was quiet in the area until a black Chevy drove slowly down the street. Dunn took note of it and trained his field glasses on the occupants. There were two men in the front seat, none in the back. *'Out cruising I guess,'* Gil thought to himself as he drained the last sip of water from his liter of bottled water.

The Chevy continued down the street until it passed a side street. It then stopped and backed up staying in the middle of the street. Dunn got renewed interest in this car. Blue Jay was about one block up that side street and walking toward the Chevy.

Dunn swung the laser pointed at the picture window, aimed it at the windshield of the Chevy, and held the earphone up to his right ear. Gil's eyes got wide as he dropped the earphones and picked up the com unit.

"Blue Jay," Gil yelled into the com, "go back, there are two psychos' in a black Chevy that are planning to blow you away for kicks."

Dunn got no reply from Blue Jay or Bean.

'They must have taken off their com units,' Dunn figured as he grabbed a roll of duct tape and headed for the door.

The Chevy was not in Blue Jay's view as he approached the main street, but the two inside were waiting. One in the backseat with a shotgun and the other behind the wheel with the car in gear ready for a fast departure. Blue Jay was almost to the street when he heard four muffled pops. Knowing that sound he drew his weapon and moved to see what was going on. A little further down the street, Bean was doing the same.

When both men reached the street they couldn't believe their eyes. Dunn was walking alongside a black Chevy with his hand on the steering wheel, keeping it from going to the curb. The two men quickly joined Gil who informed them, "Just out walking my Chevy."

The duo quickly figured out what happened. One man in the back with a shotgun, the other down on the front seat, and the car, having an automatic transmission, moving on its own.

"Steer this for me will you?" Dunn asked Bean.

When Bean had control of the wheel, Dunn put his .38 revolver back into his right hand and started to remove the duct tape that was holding the liter water bottle in place.

"Poor man's silencer," Dunn whispered.

Blue Jay and Bean knowingly shook their heads.

With the bottle and tape removed from the end of his .38, Gil put his weapon away then announced he is going to dispose of the bottle. Bean looked at Blue Jay and said, "You go with Gil, I'll dump this a few blocks away. It'll be chalked up as just another street gang thing."

That said, everyone turned to their tasks.

When all three had returned to the surveillance apartment, nothing was said about the incident with the Chevy. The mission and how close the turd came to discovering Blue Jay were discussed as they packed up their gear and put the laser bug back into its case.

That done Blue Jay inquired, "What is the game plan for giving surveillance back to Di Flipi?"

"Di plans to be here around six in the morning and one of his teams at eight," Dunn answered, "You and Bean can head out if you want. I don't want to leave that equipment here unattended."

"We'll stay until Di shows up," Blue Jay said.

An uneasy quiet set in for a few minutes before Blue Jay blurted out, "Guess you saved my life, Gil."

"No problem," Dunn replied, "You can do the same for me if JJ finds out about this."

"Oh shit," Bean exclaimed. "Don't even think about it. You'll give us bad luck."

All three laughed out loud, but knew there would be hell to pay if JJ and the Board found out.

When all was quiet again, Blue Jay returned to the topic.

"I would like to do something to repay you."

"Look, first of all," Gil began, "I'm the one that got you two involved in this. And second, you would have done the same for me or Bean or anyone. So forget it. I'd rather not discuss it anymore."

"I would like to ask Bean a question concerning the mission," Gil continued.

"What's that?" asked Bean.

"If you saved someone's life how do you think they could repay you?" inquired Gil.

"I knew you were going to say something like that," Blue Jay exploded.

"Like what?" Dunn asked with a smile, "I'm just asking Bean a question."

"I think he feels bad," offered Bean, "about you saving his life and him thinking about all of those times he called you Fuck Face Dunn when you were our boss at CIA."

"Did he really?" Gil inquired, already knowing the answer.

"I don't hear any noise, did he pass out or something?" asked Bean.

"No, I didn't pass out you fucking traitor," Blue Jay responded, as he started pacing back and forth, "Why don't you just give his ass a big smooch while you're at it."

"Oh no, he's pacing," Bean observed, "You know what that means."

"What's that Navy term," Gil added, "batten down the hatches, there's a storm a brewing?"

"Well, here's another term, fuck you," Blue Jay erupted, "Fuck you both."

"Now I have to go through life knowing Gilbert saved my life and he's going to rub it in every time he gets a chance with the help of any ass smoocher that may be in the area."

Blue Jay continued pacing and talking while Bean and Gil enjoyed a laughing fit.

It seemed like they just closed their eyes when they heard Di Flipi knocking on the door. It was 6 A.M. and by 6:15 Di was debriefing the three men about the operation.

At 7:00 Dunn, Bean and Blue Jay were preparing to leave.

"We'll keep the camera with us," Dunn announced. "In a neighborhood like this you might get mugged and I'm sure none of us want to lose this camera."

"We will be waiting for you about a block away," Dunn

continued. "You can follow us to my house. We'll review the Key to make sure it's what you need, then we are due for some R & R.

"Okay," Di Flipi agreed.

Since it was his operation, Dunn handed the camera to Di Flipi when they all arrived at his house, then guided him to a PC in the den.

Di hooked up the digital camera and reviewed the pictures of the key.

"Looks good," he confirmed as he printed off several copies of each picture." You all have done a great job."

"You have no idea, Di me lad," Dunn said as he put his arm over Di Flipi's shoulders, "Did we tell you about the Chevy?"

"Am I going to need a drink after hearing about it?" Di inquired.

"Maybe," Was Gil's one-word answer as he guided Di Flipi towards the liquor cabinet.

CHAPTER SIX

One month had passed since their mission and everything seemed to have worked out well. No contact from Dunn meant Di Flipi was happy and there were no other complications.

Blue Jay, Bean, and the other Team members were working hard at the Barn preparing for the big project and starting to build up their physical conditioning and stamina to the next level.

This morning was cross terrain repelling with a twist. One end of a rope had been secured to the back of a pickup truck that was parked at the base of what used to be the Barn's silo. The other end was tied off at the security position inside the top of the silo.

Blue Jay was instructing the first two men at the top of the silo on how to use a device for the rappel.

He first demonstrated how to separate the two handles, position the two small wheels over the rope, then secure and lock the handles back into their original position.

"Now you are in position," Blue Jay instructed, "Grab the handles and you are ready to go. One last thing," Blue Jay added, "this unit has a breaking device. It will hold you in place before starting and can help you control your descent, but if you are going full speed I wouldn't engage it or one of two things will happen. It will slow you down very quickly or it will be so fast you will probably do a series of backward rolls on your way to the ground. You release the brake by pressing this lever between the two handles with your thumb.

If you press a little you descend slowly. Press hard and you'll look like Superman flying through the air. When you get toward the bottom slowly ease up on the thumb pressure and it will slow your descent for landing. Any questions?" Blue Jay inquires.

"Who the fuck thought this one up?" Air Jockey inquired.

"I think it was Bean," Blue Jay answered. He always took the heat for his ideas, but since Bean sided with Dunn at the humor-fest, "Yeah take it up with Bean. He'll probably deny it though."

"Other questions?" Blue Jay asked. With no additional questions Blue Jay then hung out the silo door and yelled, "ready up here."

Bean acknowledged and instructed Check, the driver of the pick-up, to pull ahead slowly. As the truck moved away from the silo the rope unwound from the back of the truck. Once the rope was unwound it started to raise off the ground, higher and higher until it was pulled tight between the truck and the top of the silo.

When this was completed Blue Jay reached out, grabbed the rope, and gave it a few good yanks. Satisfied it was secure he inquired, "Who's first?"

"I'll go," Panda volunteered, "I have to piss anyway."

"Well, try not to piss on the way down," Blue Jay requested.

Panda's descent was perfect and Blue Jay wasn't surprised. This was just a refresher for most of the Team anyway.

"You're up," Blue Jay informed Jockey.

Air Jockey moved toward the rope, but he wasn't happy. "How did I get elected for this training?" he inquired, "Remember me, I'm the pilot, I fly things."

"Oh, you'll be flying, only this time you'll be flying yourself through the air," Blue Jay said reassuringly.

"Oh that's funny, real funny," Jockey replied, as he attached the device to the rope.

"Now remember about the break," Blue Jay instructed.

Jockey acknowledged then pressed his thumb against the break release and he was off. It wasn't pretty, but he was moving at a fast rate of speed down the rope.

As Jockey approached the end of the ride he realized he was going too fast, then remembered about the break, but forgot the part about how to slow down.

Removing his thumb completely from the break lever, the device brought Jockey's forward movement to a screeching halt. He had a death grip on the handles, but as his body moved forward and his legs got up around head high, he lost it and his body continued a complete turn and he landed in the back of the truck. Luckily when Benz put in the Judo floor he had some mats

42

left over and used them to pad the back of the truck.

Seconds after Jockey landed, Bean is standing over him and asked, "You all right?"

"Yeah, I'm okay," Jockey replied not fully recovered yet.

"Well I'll give you low marks for the ride down,"

Bean remarked, "but that back flip dismount deserves a perfect 10."

Hearing that remark Jockey made a full recovery and jumped to his feet. "Hey," Jockey exploded, "I signed on to fly, not for this Jungle Jim shit."

"Well, you were flying weren't you?" Bean asked, then looked at the Team members standing in the area and inquired, "Didn't it look like he was flying to you?"

All of the Team members agreed it looked like he was flying to them, then Panda added, "He looked like Superman with a bad hangover."

Jockey realized he couldn't get into a verbal battle with the entire Team so he singled out Bean. Besides, Blue Jay told him this whole idea was Beans'.

"Very funny, very funny," Jockey replied then focused on Bean,

"How in the fuck did you come up with this bull shit idea?" Jockey inquired.

Bean's face showed mixed emotions of laughing and confusion until Blue Jay yelled down from the silo, "Get'em, Jockey." Then he realized someone had been giving this pitbull some bad scoop. *'I wonder who that someone could be?'* Bean thought as he flipped the bird to the bird at the top of the silo.

Bean realized it was a waste of time denying anything, so he admitted to the deed and added something to make things worse. "Some of you fly boys are real prima donnas. What was that JC asked you on that Project in Mexico, "Where did you learn to fly, Pussy Airways?"

That really put Jockey into high gear, but Bean didn't care. His group was next to take the ride. He was heading for the silo and knew Jockey would not be eager to follow him to the top.

Since the Team would be deep in an unfriendly country their timing, speed and reflexes could and probably would come into play, so Benz and Panda conducted daily one hour Martial Arts training to sharpen up the Team in these areas. Classes covered hand-to-hand combat, silent killing, Karate and of course Judo.

It was Monday afternoon and a Judo class was in session with Benz and Panda moving around on the mat with Jockey and Bean.

Mac was on his way to the como shack and had stopped to watch the training.

"I'm surprised they've selected Judo for part of their training schedule," Mac said to Blue Jay who was taking a breather on the side of the mat.

"It's a good reflex and speed builder," Blue Jay answered, "It even helps speed up your thought processes, sometimes even when you're upside down in mid-air."

"You mean they're that fast?" Mac inquired.

"The Team has developed a rating system," Tic offered as he moved closer to Mac and Blue Jay. "If you can hold your own with Panda, you move on to challenge Benz. If you manage to hold your own with Benz, you wait for the next thunderstorm and try to catch lightning in this," Tic informed Mac as he held up an empty bottle.

"That quick?" replied Mac as he became more interested in the four people on the mat.

It was Jockey's turn for the daily workout with Benz. As they moved around the mat Jockey was looking for an opening to attack when Benz attempted a foot sweep. Jockey managed to recover, but didn't realize it would be followed by an uchimatti that put him in mid-air while he was still thinking about the foot sweep recovery. Jockey made a safe break fall with the help of Benz and inquired, "Did I mention I signed on as pilot, you know, to fly things?"

Benz, still holding onto the sleeve of Jockey's Judo Gi looked down with a smile on his face and inquired, "Well, you were just flying, weren't you?"

"Looked like he was flying to me," the other Team members confirmed from the side of the mat.

"I hate this job," Jockey replied as Benz helped him to his feet.

"You love it." Benz suggested with a laugh as the two men continued.

"I see what you mean," Mac observed, "Too bad my Judo Gi is in the laundry or I would have a go with Benz."

"Here Mac," Tic said as he offered him the empty bottle.

"You think I'm up to catching lightning in a bottle?"

"No," Tic replied, "use the bottle when you realize what you just said so you don't piss your pants."

"That's funny," Mac replied with smile as he leaves the area saying, "I'm going to the laundry."

JJ and the board were also very busy on this one, preparing collateral support for the Team, like long-range transportation, equipment, etc.

The Board would also be involved in this one and would take up residence closer to the Project in case they were needed. They had also developed contingency plans in case the Team got into big trouble. With Dunn, Mac and Foxie's intelligence and military connections, and the remainder of the Board's business contacts, they should be able to muster some support, but only if absolutely necessary.

Already the dollars spent were adding up, but no one on the Board was complaining. They realized it was required and a lot more would be spent for the execution of the Project.

Another week had passed and training was progressing on schedule. Besides honing their expert skills, the Team members were learning new skills. Even Jockey had mastered the thumb break release.

Everyone was in the Team meeting room attending one of Check's daily language classes when Blue Jay's beeper started to vibrate. He looked puzzled as he removed it from his belt to check the number on the display. Besides his answering service, not many people knew this beeper number. As Blue Jay focused in on his beeper's display, Bean's beeper also started to vibrate. When he looked in Blue Jay's direction, Blue Jay was already looking at him. Both men moved quietly toward the door and left the room.

All of this had not gone unnoticed by Check and the other Team members, but they figured it must be something important and they would be told if necessary.

Once outside the room Blue Jay and Bean started to discuss who beeped them.

"I got beeped by Mims," Blue Jay informed Bean.

"Jesse beeped me," Bean replied.

"Not good," Blue Jay said. "Let's get to a land line."

With that the two men headed to where the cars are parked and got into Blue Jay's Z-28. This was going to be their fastest ride to Stockton then across the bridge to Center Bridge PA.

As the duo burned up the small winding country road, their memories wondered back to the early 90s when they were recruited and trained by two senior CIA Operatives, Jar Head and Doggie. Their relationships started off well and just got better over the years.

When Jar Head married Mims and Doggie married Jesse, their Section Chief at the Agency, Swabbie was the best man, but Blue Jay and Bean were in the wedding party.

The relation had become so close between the four that the DDO used to refer to them as Blue Jay and Bean's Agency Fathers.

The fond memories brought smiles to their faces, but as they approached the Stockton city limits, their thoughts returned to why they were being beeped.

At the Stockton Inn the Z-28 turned left and headed for the river bridge that crossed the Delaware river. The car came off the bridge and seconds later Blue Jay was turning into a custard stand parking lot and stopped next to a phone booth.

Bean waited in the car as Blue Jay called Mims to see why she beeped him. The conversation got quite lengthy and Bean knew it wasn't all good.

When Blue Jay returned to the car he announced, "We got trouble."

"Figured that," Bean answered, "How bad?"

"Bad enough," Blue Jay replied, "Doggie and Jar Head went and got themselves taken hostage."

"Hostage!" Bean exclaimed, "Is there a ransom?"

"Us," Blue Jay said as he pointed to Bean and then himself.

"Is that all?" Bean acknowledged.

"It gets better. Remember back in 93 when we took out that turd on Sardinia?"

"Yeah," Bean answered.

"Well the Turd had a son at school in Europe and now he is a self-styled revolutionary and with the help of his father's money, he's trying to make a name for himself. He said to avenge his father's death he wants only us. He promises to let Jar Head and Doggie go in exchange for you and me."

"Who's he trying to shit?" Bean asked. "Doggie and Jar Head were also in on that operation and as soon as that son-of-a-turd gets all four of us in hand we're goners."

"Ya think?" Blue Jay asked knowing Bean was right.

"How are we going to handle this?" Bean inquired, "We have to go, but what about the Team and the Project?"

"I know," Blue Jay answered wondering himself what they should do.

The two men discussed how they would proceed during the drive back to the Barn. JC, the Team, JJ, and Mac were all at the Barn today. That was good because they had no time to waste. Upon arrival at the Barn, Blue Jay first stopped by the house. Bean went in and asked JJ and Mac to attend a meeting he and Blue Jay had called.

Blue Jay continued to the Barn to do the same with JC and the Team.

Ten minutes later everyone was in the Team meeting room with looks of concern on their faces. They didn't know what the meeting was about, but would bet it wasn't good.

Blue Jay and Bean were standing in front of the room and when everyone was seated Blue Jay began, "Sorry about calling this meeting on such short notice, but Bean and I have a personal problem we have to deal with ASAP. Without going into too much detail, here is the situation." "Back in the early 90's Bean and I were recruited for the Agency by two Senior Operatives, code names Jar Head and Doggie, with the idea of replacing them upon their retirement. They personally took charge of our Agency training in addition to our initial field operations and a strong bond was formed between the four of us. Some have even referred to them as our Agency Fathers."

"That was a good call on someone's part," Bean assured everyone at the meeting. "The bond is that strong. They have put their lives on the line for us and we have done the same for them. After Doggie, Jar Head, our section Chief, and the DDO retired, we also parted company with the Agency and went private. That very quick review brings us to the situation we now face."

With that said Bean turned the meeting back over to Blue Jay.

"Now for the problem," Blue Jay started, "Early on in our Agency careers, accompanied by our Agency Fathers, we were sent to Sardinia to take out a combination arms/drug dealer that would sell to anyone for the right amount, but when terrorists became his clients, he went on the hit list. This guy had a big security force, but we managed to take him out and with the help of a Seal Team made our escape. Another thing this guy had was a son attending school in Europe. The son is now a, revolutionary want-to-be that no one seems to take seriously. With the help of his old man's money he has set out to correct that and has declared he will avenge his father by exterminating the killers from the CIA and that would be Bean and I. Our guess is they could not find us or more likely thought it would be too costly to try, so they passed on us and instead, while holding guns to their wives' heads, abducted Doggie and Jar Head. Now the son-of-a-Turd wants to make a trade, us for them. We know this is bull shit and that he will kill all four of us if we agree, so we'll go with plan B."

"We realize this has been short and sweet, but we are pressed for time. I'm sure there are questions." Blue Jay offers.

The first question was fired off by JJ, "What about the Project we have in progress? We cannot execute it without you two."

"Bean and I realize that, are very sorry, and will continue with it if we are still around, and if it is okay with all of you," Blue Jay answered.

"Can this be handled any other way?" JC inquired.

"Afraid not," Bean answered, "this turd wants us."

"Let me share something with you," Bean continued, "There is more than just a relationship we are talking about here. After Blue Jay and I had a few missions completed, with the help of Jar Head and Doggie, we were scheduled to take the next one on our own. When it did come Jar Head and Doggie smelled a setup and took the mission before we knew about it. They were right about the setup and it almost got them killed. We figure if they did that for us, can we do any less?"

The room stayed quiet for a few seconds then JJ broke the silence. "JC," JJ announced as he started another question. "What are our options? How will this affect the schedule? Can we replace Blue Jay and Bean?"

"The schedule is not set in cement and can be changed up until we start operations." JC responded, "As for replacing these two, we have the Team operating like a well-oiled machine. If we try to replace two men at this point it will set us back months, plus I'm sure the Team itself will be affected."

JJ sat and pondered the situation then spoke. "First of all, I wish you both well on your mission and when you return you are welcome to come back.

Second, I'll call an emergency meeting of the Board to see what they want to do. They may want to stop operations for a while or just stop everything. To date we have put a dent in the terror network and they may want to call it a day, especially if we lose one or two members of the Team."

That said, JJ stood, approached Blue Jay and Bean, and wished them God's speed. Mac was the second to wish the duo well, then he accompanied JJ as they departed to arrange an emergency meeting of the Board.

As the two men departed JJ noticed JC and the Team stayed seated. He assumed they were stunned, disappointed, or had additional questions. Maybe they wanted to give the duo names of people they could contact to help them out on their quest.

Ron Wootters

Whatever the reason, JJ had a feeling after the Board met, this would be the last time the team would be meeting.

CHAPTER SEVEN

All of the Board members, with the exception of Gil Dunn, were seated around the conference table at JJ's suite of offices in Manhattan. JJ was briefly explaining the reason for the meeting while they are waiting for Dunn to arrive.

The Board were discussing the situation when Dunn finally arrived, "Sorry to keep you all waiting," Gil apologized as he found his seat at the far end of the table.

"I was just explaining briefly the reason for the meeting and why we will be taking a critical vote this afternoon," JJ explained, "Now that you are here I will get into more detail."

As JJ started his detailed explanation, Dunn interrupted, "I'm afraid I'll have to disqualify myself from any voting and temporarily remove myself from the Board."

'Two bomb shells in one day,' JJ thought as he immediately inquired, "What is the reason Gil?"

"My guess is the same reason you called this meeting, Jar Head and Doggie?"

"Have Blue Jay or Bean been in touch with you?" Mac inquired.

"No," Dunn answered, "it was a retired CIA Section Chief, code named Swabbie."

"Let me explain," Gil continued. "When we were young and just starting our careers at the Agency, Doggie, Jar Head, Swabbie, and myself were field operatives. Working individually or as a team we put in a good many years in the field. Swabbie and I being married and getting a little old for the field, decided to go in-house and into management. Jar Head and Doggie stayed in the field and worked as a team."

"So you're saying you are getting involved with the rescue attempt because you all worked together at one time?" JJ inquired.

"That plus they saved my ass a few times," Gil quickly replied, "One time I was in a similar situation. I was assigned to a

U.S. Embassy and a few jerks from a revolutionary group decided to take a hostage and make demands. Knowing the spooks usually have the office with the air conditioner, they recruited one of the clean-up crew to spot one and I was elected."

"Four of them pulled me off the main street and then made demands. That current administration couldn't figure out what to do and it didn't really matter because I was a goner anyway"

"Jar Head and Doggie were in transit when they got the word about the kidnapping and were in country the next day trying to find out where I was being held. It didn't take them long to find out and when the word came back down that nothing was to be done, due to diplomatic reasons, Jar head and Doggie took it upon themselves to perform the rescue."

"Since they went against orders they probably would have been in for it, but all was forgiven after someone, Swabbie, dropped a line to the New York Times about the heroic CIA rescue of an Embassy employee."

"How do you plan to pull this off?" Mac inquired, "Even if you team up with Bean and Blue Jay there will only be three of you."

"There is something you may not know," Gil replied, "Blue Jay, Bean, Jar Head and Doggie's Section Chief was Swabbie. Swabbie reported directly to me; I was the DDO. We'll think of something."

There was so much to consider. The Board wanted more time to consider everything and decided to meet again early the next morning.

JJ and Mac were back at the house in Jersey when JC entered the room. "You tried to warn me about how Blue Jay might go off on some crusade and take people with him," Mac said to JC. "We will be losing two, but that's better than the whole Team," Mac continued.

"That's not entirely true," JC corrected Mac. "The entire Team has elected to go and hope you two and the Board will understand."

"And if we don't?" JJ inquired.

"Its been nice." JC replied.

"What do you have to say about all of this?" Mac asked JC.

"Its been very nice," JC answered.

"You mean you're going too?" Mac exploded.

"I'm the Team leader," JC reminded Mac, "Can't let them go on something like this without me."

"It just gets better and better," JJ observed, "The Team, then the Board, then the Team again. I suppose you will want to go, too?" JJ motioned toward Mac.

"Do miss those rides on the jet with the Team and guarding the air craft when they are away," Mac answered.

Both JJ and JC had known Mac for many years and could tell when he was kidding and this time he was not kidding.

"Just fucking shoot me!" JJ requested, as he stood and walked over to the window.

"What's the game plan?" Mac inquired.

"The Team is kicking that around right now," JC answered.

"Okay wait a minute," JJ announced, as he turned away from the window. "I just took a quick count, myself, and four other board members are the only ones that haven't lost their minds, but since majority rules, count me in as well. I'll contact three of the members, they may or may not join us, but if not we'll make do."

"Mac," JJ continued, "since Foxie is new to the Board and a friend of yours, maybe you should contact him?"

"Good idea," Mac agreed, "I'll assure him this is not our SOP."

"You better tell the Team," JJ instructed JC. "With more resources available it will probably change their planning."

As JJ moved toward the phone, he looked at Mac and inquired, "Why am I doing this? I think it's from being around you, you're a bad influence."

"Ya think?" Mac replied then added, "You know, maybe we can swing by Cuba on the way and borrow those fifty caliber rifles we gave to Charley Tuna?"

"Fuck you," was JJ's two-word reply.

All of the Board members were in agreement and it was a go for everyone.

This situation would be conducted like any other Project except for the planning; that would be on a super rush schedule.

The Team and Board had put aside the current big Project they were all working on and had picked up this new urgent one.

Early the next morning, while the others members of the Board were planning transportation, logistical support, etc., Foxie and Dunn were gathering Intel.

Since the abductor's instructions were for Blue Jay and Bean to come to Corsica to exchange themselves for the freedom of their friends, the Board and Team knew two things: Where Doggie and Jar Head were and if this guy was anything like his father, he had a huge security force.

Knowing the location, Foxie contacted his sources at Navy Intel and the Sixth Fleet. Dunn called Di Flipi who already knew about the abduction and started research knowing Dunn would be calling.

The Team were planning the operation and referred to it as a KISS Project, (Keep It Simple, Stupid). With such short notice and going up against who knows what, the plan had to be simplicity itself.

JC had been jumping between attending the planning and doing something in the Com shack?

That night the Team were once again in session, this time to review all of the information that had been gathered about the abductor's home base on Corsica, especially his security force.

Bean was busy reviewing Intel and remarked, "It looks like he has three times the security force his father had," he said as he passed the documents to Blue Jay.

After scanning the documents Blue Jay replied, "Well, we almost have three times as many on our side."

"Yeah I know, but last time the odds were ten to one in their favor," Bean laughed.

"A slight technicality," Blue Jay said with a smile.

"What are these children getting us into?" Mac inquired out

54

loud, as he reached for more documents to review.

"Here is one thing that may be in our favor," Bris offered, "His compound is on the east coast. We may be able to make use of that."

Everyone was still reading the documents when JJ arrived from the Board meeting.

"How are things progressing?" he inquired.

"Reviewing Intel right now," JC informed him, "and a new type of plan has been developed called, The Floating Simplicity."

"How does it work?" JJ inquired.

"We're not sure, but we all agree we'll know it when we see it," offered Blue Jay.

"It's sort of like, if shit happens we'll go with it and if it doesn't we'll do something else," JC confirmed.

"I see," JJ said as he looked at Mac.

"Don't ask me," said Mac sensing JJ's stare, "he's getting as bad as the rest of them."

If the Team was sitting around the dinner table that would have been the shot that started one of their Bull Shit Derbies, but under these circumstances everyone just smiled and kept reading.

"While you are reviewing the documents, I'll catch you all up on what we have in place," said JJ. "First of all the jet is ready to go and the second prop aircraft is being ferried into position. Arrangements were made for the additional weapons you requested to be delivered to the freight area of the airport, we'll pick them up there. We have also managed to get use of a villa on the coast about five miles from the objective. It is in a very rural area, but you know how those rich people are about their privacy." JJ continued until he had covered everything on his list. There would be more information, but be relayed as it came in.

"What about the case of flares?" JC inquired.

"It will be waiting in the freight area," JJ assured him.

Seeing there were no other questions he inquired to Blue Jay about the time situation.

"Swabbie is stalling the abductors with things like *'he cannot locate us'* and *'you know the kind of business they are in, they could be anywhere,'* but the abductors are getting impatient."

"Do we have a timetable?" JJ inquired.

"We figure tomorrow morning we'll move closer to Corsica," Blue Jay volunteered. "JC has rigged up communications so we can communicate with Swabbie and you from over there."

After a few seconds of quiet, Panda mumbled in a low, but loud enough voice, so all can hear, "Another fucking prop aircraft." Then in a louder voice said, "Who will be flying the prop aircraft sir?"

"I hope it's not you know who," Jockey added.

"At least I didn't learn how to fly at Pussy Airways," JC said, defending his flying skills.

"Spare us," Panda said. "General Mac, did we ever tell you about the Project in Mexico and that prop aircraft?" Panda asked.

"I think the tale was started a few times, but I never really got the whole story."

"Ah, they're all pussies, Mac." JC again defended himself with a big smile on his face as he gathered additional Intel for the morning briefing.

JJ could tell by the conversation that Team was ready and prayed all would return safely.

CHAPTER EIGHT

At 3 A.M. the following morning the Team was enjoying a hardy breakfast Top and the Ladies had prepared for them and by four they were seated in the Team classroom. JC entered and proceeds to the front of the room. "Good morning men," he greeted the sleepy-eyed Team.

"Morning," a few replied."

"I'm going to cover what we have on Intel and again review the game plan. We will cover any additional info en route, but that's nothing new we've done that before."

The Team members shook their heads in agreement like it was no big deal and JC continued. "First of all, we all know the What and Why for this Project, but I think the bad guy needs a code name. How about SOT, for son-of-turd?" JC offered.

"Sounds good," is the general consciences.

"Now here are the Who," JC informed the group as he passed out two pieces of paper to each member. "These are recent pictures of Jar Head and Doggie that Swabbie faxed to us. These are the only two faces at the compound we will consider as friendly's."

"Now for the Where," JC continued as he motioned everyone to join him at a table at the front of the room.

"We already know the objective is in the southern part of Corsica. The compound is located on top of a small cliff overlooking a cove in the Mediterranean Sea.

JC pointed to photos on the table that must have come out of someone's file somewhere?

"After the old man was eliminated, SOT returned to their home in Sardinia and tried to keep the old man's business going, but due to his inexperience and the heat put on the business by the U.S. and Italian governments, SOT kept the home in Sardinia, but moved the business to the island of Corsica. As you all know, it is the island right next to Sardinia, but is under French rule. If things get too hot in Corsica, he scrambles back to the Sardinia compound.

"Apparently no one really takes the little bastard seriously, but he has been making money hand over fist in the drug and weapons market and will sell to anyone including terrorists. He is also a member and big supporter of the National Front for the Liberation of Corsica and the NFLC wants home rule and are responsible for assassinations and terrorist activities for years."

"It sounds like this guy should have been on someone's radar screen a long time ago," Benz offered.

"I agree," JC continued, "I think it may have something to do with no one taking him seriously. His competitors allowed him to grow and Intel didn't think he was any kind of threat."

"However, there is a rumor the French Foreign Legion units stationed on Corsica would like to put an end to SOT and his gang of thugs."

"That would be a good group to have on our side," Bris said wishfully.

"We're working on it," JC quickly replied, and then continued the briefing.

"We will all continue to review the Intel during the flight over, but now let's fast forward to How."

"We hope Doggie and Jar Head are being held in the compound we just reviewed, due to it being the most secure of his holdings. We say he's a Turd, but we didn't say he was a stupid Turd. He or people around him will think Blue Jay and Bean will try something, but with such short notice be expecting only two men, not nine. It would be ten, but Air Jockey will be flying that day."

"As long as it's not down a fuckin' rope," Jockey replied then continued with, "heard every word, just resting my eyes."

"Just checking," JC quipped, then announced, "Now let's see if I understand this Floating Simplicity Plan,"

"Oh joy," Panda remarked, "He came up with the idea and even named it. Can we leave now? I don't want to miss any of the action in Corsica."

"Okay, I think I've got it," JC said with a smile.

"I don't like it," Panda objected, "He had that same smile on his face the night he blew the shit out of that plane with all of those terrorists on it."

"Nooo," JC corrected, "that was a different smile."

Now that JC had the Team totally awake, they would start reviewing the plan.

At the same time JC was conducting the briefing Gil Dunn was at his home putting the finishing touches on an idea JC proposed. JC has had close ties with the French Foreign Legion for many years. With all of his ribbons, jump wings, and just his manner, they adopted him as one of their own many years ago when he was still a Captain in the Marine Corps.

JC had already set up the first part and Dunn was working on part two. Already having a secure line set up so he and the Frenchman could communicate without being detected, Dunn felt free to talk.

"I need someone recalled from Corsica," Dunn requested.

"How soon?" the Frenchman asked.

"Now," Dunn answered.

After a brief pause the Frenchman offered, "It sounds like using the media and something to do with terrorists."

"That's good," Dunn approved, "and make sure the unnamed source mentions big buck payoffs to high French government officials."

"How high?"

"The top," Gil answered.

"Who is to be recalled from Corsica?" the Frenchman inquired.

Gil explained the who, how and how much, but never the why and the Frenchman knew better than to ask. If he was required to know he would be told. That was why their relationship had lasted for so many years.

Two hours later JC had completed the briefing and he was meeting with JJ and Mac at the house prior to departure. Mac would be leaving with the Team and JJ would be staying at home base with Top and the Ladies, or so the Team thought. The Board would be taking up residence at a villa on Corsica five miles from the SOT compound. The members of this Board were not the usual types of Board members. When JJ chose them he knew that, but he has had his hands full keeping them from getting too close to the action and after the Washington, D.C. emergency Project he gave up trying."

"They all feel that if they are asking people to perform extremely dangerous projects, they should be close enough to the action to help in any way they can."

JJ, Mac and JC have completed their brief meeting and were on their way back to the Barn.

Top had CNN on the TV and as the three men walked through the kitchen they heard, "Unnamed sources claim French Liaison on Corsica linked to Terrorist and extremely high level corruption in the French government."

"Works for me," JC said to JJ and Mac as he opened the kitchen door and proceeded to the Barn.

The Team and Mac had been going over Intel and the plan during the flight and the business jet was on final approach at a remote airstrip on Sardinia. The runway was almost unusable for jet aircraft, but Air Jockey made do.

"Good job," his co-pilot JC approved as the jet taxied close to the prop aircraft parked next to the only building at the strip.

"Even for somebody that flew for Pussy Airways?" Jockey inquired.

"Especially for somebody that flew for Pussy Airways," JC reassured Jockey as both men started to laugh.

When the jet came to a stop, the team wasted no time in unloading the plane. Two M-60 machine guns, ammo, a box of smoke & gas grenades, and the flares went to the prop aircraft. Parachutes, spare chutes, the .50 caliber rifles, a box of frag grenades and everything else were taken to the building. Before they lost daylight the chutes were taken to a grassy area, unpacked, checked, and re-packed. That done, weapons check was the next item.

While Blue Jay and the Team were busy preparing, JC and Mac were in communications with JJ and Swabbie while Jockey checked out the prop aircraft.

'It isn't the latest model, but it's in good shape.' Jockey thought as he looked around the aircraft.

After doing a physical inspection, he fired up the two props. Setting the brake he stood on the foot brake and revved up the engines until the wings on the aircraft were almost flapping like a bird. Satisfied everything was in proper working order, he shut down the engines and set to his next task, the M-60s.

Picking up one of the M-60s, Jockey moved to the back of the rear compartment, swung the bi-pod down, and placed the M-60 on the floor of the plane.

After putting the end of the muzzle as close to the rear ramp as possible, he then placed a nylon seat harness by the end of the stock at the other end of the weapon.

He then retrieved a rope with a carabineer secured to one end and after attaching the carabineer to the seat harness, secured the other end of the rope to the front of the cabin. That done he repeats the process for the other M-60, then secures a longer rope and carabineer to the front of the cabin.

After checking to make sure the ropes and harnesses would support the weight of a man, Jockey picked up the M-60 machine guns by their carrying handles and headed for the building to join the rest of the team.

Blue Jay and Bean were now handling communications and when Jockey entered the building JC and Mac approached him and took charge of the weapons.

"Remember how these work?" JC asked Mac.

"Yes, and if I don't, I'll just muddle through," Mac said then added, "did I ever tell you I liked you better when you were a Captain?"

"Once or twice," JC replied with a smile.

"Just checking to make sure," Mac answered. "Do the bullets come out here?" he asked as he pointed to the end of the barrel.

"They do and they are called ROUNDS!" JC corrected.

"OH! ROUNDS," Mac repeated.

The Team members laughed as the two continued their

verbal jousting as they broke down the machine guns for inspection and cleaning. With the exception of Jamaica, Mac and JC were not usually with the team during the fire fights, but the Team members had no concerns about them keeping up their end.

As the two continued inspecting and cleaning the weapons, Mac kept asking questions he already knew the answers to and JC was correcting him like a proper school master.

The Team listened and laughed while attending to their own duties. The scene resembled the 1940s when people listened to the radio while doing chores around the house.

———

With Jeff Dawson piloting a second business jet the Board was airborne a few hours after the Team departed and were on final approach at Ajaccio-Campo Airport on Corsica.

Arrangements had been made for a small yacht to be available and upon landing, JJ and the Board would proceed to the coast and sail the yacht up to the remote villa they rented; just six super rich Americans throwing their money away on a whim.

Once the cover for the yacht was established JJ and Admiral Fox would wait until early the next morning, then sail the yacht up the coast to within two miles of the SOT compound. There was a deserted Villa with a dock big enough to handle the yacht. It was owned by a member of the super rich, but between the NFLC and the high crime rate on the island, they gave it up and moved on to another island.

CHAPTER NINE

It was four AM the following morning and the two engine prop was rumbling down the remote airstrip on Sardinia. Not knowing the terrain at the jump site, it would be jump at first light. If they were detected it shouldn't cause much alarm. A French Foreign Legion Parachute Regiment were stationed on Corsica and anyone seeing the parachutes would assume they were off course and making a practice jump in the wrong area.

The plane stayed low as it navigated across the straight separating Sardinia and Corsica. As night started to become day the plane was approaching the jump zone and the rear ramp of the plane was lowered.

JC was acting as jump master and standing at the back of the plane waiting for Jockey to give the word over the plane's com unit. Blue Jay was first in line and his eyes were glued to JC. Seconds clicked by then, "Do it," came over the com unit. An instant later JC was yelling "Go, go, go, go," at the same time swinging his left arm in a large circle.

Blue Jay, followed by the other eight Team members, quickly moved to the end of the ramp and kept right on going. They were jumping at 3,000 feet and were opening quickly to give themselves more time to view the terrain before landing.

JC and Mac were still looking out the back and counting chutes as they opened. "Nine, no total or partial failures," JC announced as he pressed the handle to raise the rear ramp.

Jockey started a slow left turn that would take them back to the jump zone as JC and Mac joined him in the cockpit. As Jockey flew the plane over the Team he heard an, "All okay," over his com unit and knew the jump was successful. After dipping the left, then the right wing to the Team, Jockey continued in a straight line for a brief time, then again banked to the left and headed toward the Mediterranean Sea, but would stay close to the area.

JC and Mac were busy putting into place all of the rigging Jockey worked on last night. When special lines are secured to the M-60s, JC and Mac again joined Jockey in the cockpit.

'So far, so good,' Blue Jay thought to himself as the Team members finished burying their chutes after moving out of the landing area.

After moving on a short distance further Blue Jay halted the Team and they grouped up to break out maps and global positioning devices. Once satisfied they were in the right place, they moved out. The jump site was one mile from the objective and the team was moving very quickly to close that distance before the sun rose out of the east.

The Team had made excellent time at getting to their objective and were at an elevated wooded area 1200 yards from the SOT compound. Blue Jay quickly discussed the best positions for the .50s with Pru and Met.

Since they worked so well together in the past, Benz would be the spotter for Pru, Panda for Met, and the remainder of the Team would go with Blue Jay. Wishing each other luck, the two groups separated.

When the edge of the sun started to climb over the horizon the five members of the Team were in position on the east side of the compound. Looking back at the horizon Blue Jay waited for the right moment, then he was off to do what he does best.

Tired security guards thought they saw something moving as they looked toward the rising sun, but when they looked harder it turned out to be nothing.

Not knowing where Jar Head and Doggie were being held Blue Jay opted for starting at the lower levels of the building and working up. Finding the nearest door unlocked, Blue Jay entered and listened for any conversation or movement of any kind. Finding that all was quiet, he removed his 9mm pistol from its holster and screwed a silencer onto the end of the barrel. As he moved down a long hallway he discovered stairs that led to a lower level and another hallway. He quickly moved down the steps and at the bottom knelt down and slowly looked around the corner. Halfway down the hall was a guard seated outside a closed door. *'Must be it,'* Blue Jay thought as he stood and concealed his weapon behind his right leg, walked at a normal pace toward the guard. Between the early morning hour and the surprise of a stranger walking down the hall the guard was slow to react and was dispatched quickly.

Locating the keys to the locked room, Blue Jay gained entry and dragged the guard into the room.

"Well, it's about time," Jar Head greeted his former student.

"I'll say," Doggie chimed in, "I thought we taught them better."

Blue Jay shook his head and smiled as he discovered the keys that unlocked the shackles on their hands and feet. Shackles off, Blue Jay removed his small backpack, and opened it to produce two 9mm pistols and four full magazines.

"Okay!" Jar Head approved as he and Doggie grab the pistols and magazines. As they each chambered a round in their pistols, Doggie inquired, "Have any frags in there?"

"You and those fucking frag grenades," Blue Jay scolded, then produced two grenades.

"There's a good lad," Doggie approved.

"I didn't want you two pouting," Blue Jay informed them.

"What's the plan?" Jar Head inquired. "Shoot our way out?"

"Not yet," Blue Jay instructed as he put on his com unit and said in a low voice, "Subjects located and ready."

"Can they move on their own," Bean inquired.

"Your Father is requesting frags," Blue Jay informed him.

"That figures," Bean replied, "I'll call the plane and get things started."

Seconds later Bean was on the com again,

"Plane on the way."

While they were waiting Blue Jay explained the escape plan to Jar Head and Doggie.

When he was done the first thing out of their mouths were, "What about the little bastard that kidnapped us and how about that chopper on the roof?"

"That's not part of the plan," Blue Jay said.

"Improvise," Jar Head and Doggie recommended and started adding to the plan.

Talk about a Floating Simplicity Plan. These two and JC must have gone to the same school.

A few minutes later Blue Jay is explaining the plan to Bean,

"Do you have all of that?" Blue Jay asked.

"Yeah," Bean answered.

"Do you believe this shit?" He then inquired.

"Yeah," Bean again answered.

"Guess I do too," Blue Jay gave in then added, "the next time you come in and deal with them."

"Like that's going to make a difference," Bean replied.

"You better alert everyone about the upcoming explosions unless these old fucks get themselves and me killed beforehand."

———————

JC had lowered the rear ramp until it was even with the floor of the plane, put on his seat harness and hooked himself up to the special long line Jockey had installed for him. He then removed the top on the box of grenades to reveal a mix of smoke and gas grenades. Sitting on the deck, JC took one of the smoke grenades from its little pigeon hole in the box, removed the pull pin, and placed it back into the box so the spoon(lever) on the grenade pressed against the side of the pigeon hole and stayed in place. He continued this process for the entire box.

Mac was watching this and shook his head every time JC put a grenade back into the box.

"Where did I go wrong with your training in the Corps?" Mac inquired.

"Why?" JC asked.

"Why!" Mac erupted, "If one of the spoons on those smoke grenades gives way we'll have a shit load of smoke, but if a gas grenade goes off we'll have supped up tear gas, not to mention all of that pesky plastic flying through the air."

"It's part of the Floating Simplicity Plan," JC replied.

"If you did this kind of shit in the Corp you would probably be floating towards a Section Eight." Mac advised.

Just as Mac finished, Jockey relayed the additions to the plan.

"Floating Simplicity," JC announced. "Those guys must have gone to the same school as I did."

"More Section Eights," Mac exclaimed.

"Set up for first run," Jockey advised over the com.

Without hesitation JC stood, picked up the box of grenades, and moved out to the middle of the ramp. He then carefully set the box down and took a seat next to it.

"Get ready JC," Jockey alerted.

JC changed from a seated to a prone position, grabbed the box in the middle and extended it to the edge of the ramp so half of the box was hanging over the edge.

While waiting for the next instruction, JC took a quick look toward the ground. He realized Jockey had to come in low, but if he got any lower he'd be swapping spit with a tall tree. *'Maybe I've been too rough on the lad,'* JC wondered, then smiled as he thought, *'but this will give me ammunition for the next Bull Shit Derby.'*

"Ready!" Jockey alerted followed by, "Do it."

JC flipped the box upside down, shook it, let it go, and then rejoined Mac to prepare for the second pass.

All of the grenades fell out of the box and the spoons immediately flew off. The smoke grenades almost immediately started giving off smoke while the gas had a three to five second delay. A few of the grenades landed short or long of the compound, but the majority landed inside.

The idea was to cause confusion starting with the low flying plane, followed up with the smoke and gas.

When the plane was on approach, Bean alerted Blue Jay and the trio started making their way to the office of SOT and the copter on the roof.

Moving to the next level was no problem, but halfway down the hall on the ground floor a man came out of nowhere and was immediately taken out by two shots from Blue Jay's 9mm.

"Kids' still quick, Doggie approved.

"Just like his dad," Jar Head said with pride.

"I'm talking about shooting, not in bed," Doggie corrected.

"I see you two haven't changed much," Blue Jay observed as all three continued down the hall toward the stairs that led to

SOT's office and the chopper on the roof. The trio were halfway up the steps when the plane flew over the compound. While everyone was still looking out the windows, the three men burst into the office and took out everyone, but SOT was not among them.

"The roof," Doggie said and the three moved toward the steps leading to the roof.

By now the smoke and gas were spreading over the compound and SOT figured he had better depart. Being at the right place at the right time, he instructed his copter pilot to get in and start the engine while he instructed his bodyguards to secure the roof until he was gone.

When the trio heard the copter engine starting up they ran up the stairs and found a shit load of rounds coming their way.

"Fuck this," Jar Head announced as he pulled the pin on his frag and let the spoon fly free. After a two second hold he tossed the grenade onto the roof. After it exploded Blue Jay and Jar Head follow up with gunfire while Doggie pulled the pin on his grenade and counted, "1,000 1, 1,000 2, 1,000 3," then tossed it toward the chopper that was just lifting off.

The explosion from the grenade went up through the pilot and passenger compartment and for good measure ignited the fuel tanks causing secondary explosions. While the sound of the second explosion could still be heard, Bean was in Blue Jay's ear singing, "Wheree-aree-youuuuu?"

"On our way," Blue Jay replied as he ushered the other two down the stairs.

A few minutes later Doggie, Jar Head and Blue Jay had joined Bean and three other men wearing hooded masks to conceal their identities. Bean explained the men were members of an elite group from French Intel that try to keep their identities a secret.

Jar Head and Doggie understood and thanked the men for their help.

Bris was acting as the English speaking leader of the three-man team and said something to Tic and Check in French. They had no idea what the hell he said, but figure he was passing on the thanks and acknowledged it.

Bean held a second com unit up to his ear and inquired, "Are you close? We're ready."

"On approach," Jockey replied.

"Better get down," Bean recommended, "Something may come flying through here."

JC had lowered the back ramp as far as it would go. He and Mac hooked up their seat harnesses to the safety ropes Jockey installed and were manning the M-60 machine guns. As they approached the area Benz came on the com. "Be advised, think we saw a man with a stinger on his shoulder, but we lost him in the smoke. Will keep searching."

"Hear that back there?" Jockey inquired.

"We heard," JC replied as he reached for the small bundles of flares he had prepared and handed several to Mac.

"I heard that Crew Chiefs in helicopters used these in Nam for the same reason," Mac approved.

"Did it work?" JC asked with a smile.

"You're just getting funnier and funnier," Mac observed as he checked out the bundles of flares.

"Lock and load gentlemen, we have arrived," Jockey alerted his gunners.

JC and Mac chambered a round in their M-60s and waited.

"Ready, ready, do it," Jockey instructed as he pulled the two engine prop into a climb. As the nose of the plane rose Mac and JC started to see the tops of the trees, then the ground. When the compound came into view JC and Mac opened fire. They were not looking for accuracy, just to spray the compound and cause more confusion; they are doing a good job of it. They managed to spray the compound with .30 caliber rounds from one side to the other before they were out of range.

"Man with stinger acquired," Panda reported into the com unit as he directed Met onto the target. Within a few seconds Met had a .50 caliber round on its way, but the man had already fired the stinger.

"Stinger fired before man taken out," Panda again reported

into the com unit.

"I see it," JC announced, "Jockey bank right. Start poppin' and tossin', Mac," JC instructed, as he fired up the first bundle and tossed it out the back.

Mac didn't need to be told, his first bundle went out right behind JC's. When the bundles of flares burned, they got a lot hotter than a prop engine and the stinger decided to chase them instead.

The plane was not scheduled for another pass, but would stay in the area until the rescue was completed in case they were needed.

When the rounds from the plane stopped hitting the compound, Benz came on the com, "Time to come home," he alerted the group in the building.

The men in the building stood and moved to the door leading to the compound.

"You folks out there ready?" Bean inquired.

"Ready," Benz confirmed.

"Let's do it," Blue Jay instructed and Bris, Tic then Check moved through the door and back the way they originally came in. Once they got to some decent cover they stopped and set up for any covering fire that may be needed for the next group. Blue Jay saw they were in place and moved out the door with Jar Head and Doggie in tow and Bean covering the rear.

"So far, so good," Bris offered when the two groups met.

"Hold that thought," Blue Jay said then motioned for Bris to move out again.

This time the second group would cover the first and the .50s were watching over both groups.

When Blue Jay's group was in their second move Benz alerted, "Down a second, you have fleas behind you."

When the two groups turned to look behind them they saw two men flying through the air after being hit by the .50 caliber rounds.

"All clear," Benz notified the groups over the com.

A few more jumps and the two groups were out of immediate danger, but they were seen leaving and a big force was regrouping at the compound to give chase, but Pru and Met were slowing that process down a little.

When a man looked like he was taking charge, Met or Pru took them out and the process was stalled.

When the men in the compound finally wised up and moved behind the building, the crew figured it was time to move on.

As they prepared to move out they heard the roar of many propeller aircraft approaching the area and a short time later the first parachute of the French Foreign Legion Parachute Regiment could be seen opening, followed by another and another. By the looks of the number of planes, the entire regiment was jumping.

Faced with this new dilemma, the new leaders at the compound reasoned the entire thing was a military operation and being out-numbered decided to flee the area.

———————

Blue Jay and Bean were walking close to Jar Head and Doggie as they moved toward the rendezvous with the yacht.

"These French guys are really good," Jar Head said with approval.

"I'll say," Doggie agreed, "We should have some units this good in U.S. Intel."

"Oh, I agree," Blue Jay said approvingly, "They are the best. Don't you think so, Bean?"

"The very best," Bean confirmed.

Since the SOT Security Force was forced to disperse, the trip to the yacht was uneventful.

When they arrived at the deserted villa the Team checked out the area looking for any person or persons that may have been staking out the area. When satisfied the area was clear they all moved toward the dock and the yacht.

Since the identity of everyone was confidential, JJ and Foxie were also wearing hooded masks.

When Doggie and Jar Head boarded the yacht, they were escorted to one of the sleeping quarters to keep them isolated from the others.

The Team would also remain below decks in the galley area for the five mile trip back to the villa where the Board was staying.

Blue Jay and Bean were keeping, their Agency Fathers company during the sea cruise and all was pleasant until Jar Head asked, "Who are those people that helped rescue us?"

"I told you," Blue Jay said without hesitation, "French Intel."

"You wouldn't bull shit your old daddies, would you?" Doggie inquired.

"No, it's true," Bean insisted,

"That shit was floating pretty good until the way you both answered one of our questions," Doggie informs the duo.

"What question was that?" Blue Jay said while he and Bean prepared for battle.

"How did it go, Doggie?" Jar Head tried to remember. "Didn't we say, These French guys are really good and we should have some units this good in U.S. Intel?"

"Yeah," Doggie confirmed, "then this one said," pointing toward Blue Jay, "I agree, they are the best," then his brother added, "the very best."

"So what?" Bean got defensive.

"So," Jar Head fired off, "you two shit birds wouldn't say, the best and very best unless you belonged to the unit yourselves."

"That's not true," Blue Jay counter- attacked. "We've given credit to other units."

"Yeah," Doggie replied, "but it never got above good or very good and never, the best!"

"Maybe we haven't seen anyone as good as this French unit before," Blue Jay offered.

"They're trying to blow smoke up daddy's ass again," Jar Head announced.

The conversation went into high gear and their voices could be heard in the galley.

"Family reunions can be rough," Benz observed as he and the Team laughed while shaking their heads.

The debate had ended, but not resolved by the time the yacht was tied up at the villa's dock.

The Team was the first to disembark proceeding to the villa and a waiting van. Gil Dunn and other Board members would remain out of sight in an upstairs bedroom until Jar Head, Doggie and the Team left the area.

The Frenchman arranged to have two vans waiting at the villa. The Team would use one and the father son team the other.

When both vans were loaded they started the trip to Ajaccio-Campo Airport.

After the vans pulled out of the villa and onto the road, JJ and Foxie appeared in front of the villa and were shortly joined by the other Board members. As they watched the vans drive away JJ said, "Well, it's done. Their were times I had my doubts," he admitted.

"It was a hairy operation," Dunn agreed.

"Anyone up for a brew?" Wilson inquired.

"Sounds good," JJ admitted, "Very good."

"Have to make another call first," Dunn announced, "Pour me one."

"Have another scoop for CNN," was Dunn's first sentence into the phone.

"Yes?" the Frenchman inquired.

"Former CIA officials rescued by Elite French Intel Unit and French Foreign Legion Parachute Regiment on Corsica. The two were kidnapped last week by Corsican NFLC king pin. Daylight raid rescued the two men while eliminating the king pin and many of his security force. Financial arrangement between NFLC king pin and high French government official still unanswered."

"Is that all?" the Frenchman asked.

"No," replied Gil. "Tip CNN and the U.S. Embassy in Paris that the two former CIA officials will be at the Air France counter at Ajaccio-Campo Airport on Corsica this afternoon."

Dunn and the Frenchman discussed a few more issues then hung up.

When Dunn rejoined the others JJ handed him his drink then proposes a toast. "May all have a safe journey home."

"Safe journey home," the board members echoed as they touched glasses and then took a drink.

When the two vans got close to the airport, Blue Jay pulled into the parking lot of an upscale hotel.

"It'll be better if you get transportation to the airport from here," Blue Jay recommended, "Go to the Air France counter. There should be someone waiting, if not, call this number," Blue Jay instructed as he hands a piece of paper to Jar Head.

"Here's money for the cab and whatever else you might want," Bean said as he handed a roll of bills to Doggie.

"We'll follow at a distance until you enter the airport terminal building," Blue Jay finished.

"We want to thank you children," a grateful Jar Head said in a serious voice.

"It would have been the end for us if you hadn't showed up," an equally serious Doggie added.

Never seeing them like this before, Bean and Blue Jay were taken aback.

"No need for that," Bean assured them. "We have all been through a lot in the past."

"We don't mean to embarrass you," Jar Head assured the two. "We realize the four of us have never talked like this before, but Doggie and I just want you to know our feelings."

"Thank you," Bean and Blue Jay replied having been taken off guard by their words.

"It's a shame we couldn't thank the other members of the unit as well. Who are they anyway?"

"I knew it, I fucking knew," Blue Jay exclaimed. "We should have left these two determined fucks with that asshole at the compound."

"Tell me about it!" Bean agreed, then instructed, "get out of the van."

"We used to be agents you know," Doggie assured them. "We can be trusted."

"Yeah, but you keep getting yourselves captured," Blue Jay fired back.

"Get out of the fucking van," Bean said again.

"Let's go," Jar Head suggested as he pulled the door on the van open, "These two have graduated from shit birds to uppity shit birds."

Knowing they didn't get any info, but at least had pissed off the other two, Jar Head and Doggie laughed as they got out of the van.

As they started to walk toward the hotel entrance they scanned the parking lot looking for the other van they knew was there. They finally spotted it in the far corner of the parking lot and waved a *'thank you'* as the van's headlights turned on and off signaling a *'you're welcome'*.

The vans followed at a distance until the taxi was inside the airport grounds, then the Team van turned off and proceeded to another part of the airport.

Blue Jay and Bean followed the cab to the Air France entrance and waited until Jar Head and Doggie were inside, then left to join the rest of the Team at the jet.

After their air to ground support action, Mac, JC, and Jockey returned to the strip in Sardinia, picked up the jet, flew it to Corsica, and had been waiting for the Team.

When Blue Jay and Bean arrived at the jet everyone was seated onboard in a Semi-relaxed state. Jockey was catching a nap before the flight back to the states while Bris and JC were monitoring the media for information about the CIA kidnap victims.

As the two also boarded the plane JC informed them, "We may as well make sure they don't disappear again before we leave."

"Good idea," the two agreed as they stowed their gear in the back of the cabin and collapsed into a couple of seats.

Two hours passed before something was heard about the CIA kidnap victims. Knowing the state department had them in tow and the media was all over the story, the Jet taxied for takeoff.

———

Mac and the Team were back at the Barn that night and JJ was there the following day.

The Team usually took a month or so off after a Project, but since this was a special Project, all agreed to one week off then it was back to planning and training for the big Project.

During their time off, Bean and Blue Jay drove to Virginia to visit their old teachers. As they passed Philadelphia, Bean noticed Blue Jay is deep in thought. "Something bothering you?" Bean inquired.

"No, just fond memories from the past," Blue Jay answered,

"I use to train at Mr. Okazaki's Dojo in Philadelphia. Talk about being at the right place at the right time. Back then Mr. Okazaki was a 7th degree black belt in the Japan Karate Association and had requested Mr. Kisaka, a 4th degree, be sent to Philadelphia as assistant instructor." "Shortly after that Mr. Enoeda, a 5th degree, showed up to visit his instructor and Mr. Okazaki immediately had him instructing classes. It took some months before JKA Headquarters in Japan finally tracked Mr. Enoeda down and ordered him to proceed immediately to Europe and his new assignment."

"I can't believe how fortunate we all were!" Blue Jay exclaimed, "Black Belts of that rank in Japan usually instruct 3rd and 4th degree on up and here we were with two, sometimes all three of them instructing the same class. Of course all three are exceptional experts, but each one also had a thing they were noted for. For Mr. Okazaki it was his punching, Mr. Kisaka it was kicking and Mr. Enoeda it was his power. Think that is why they nicknamed him Tora (Tiger) in Japan? I can still hear his voice yelling, "HIPS!" during Karate class."

"It doesn't get much better than that," Bean approved.

"No it doesn't," Blue Jay agreed, "and if you wanted to study another style of Karate or were looking for top notch Judo instruction, all you had to do was drive over to Cranford, New Jersey and Mr. Yonezuka's (Yone) Judo and Karate Center. Yone is an excellent teacher, world class competitor and was twice the coach for the U.S. Olympic Judo Team."

"Would you say Yone and Benz are at the same level?" Bean inquired.

"I can honestly say the two are equal in every way," Blue Jay confirmed.

Bean and Blue Jay were attending a very small welcome home party Swabbie and Anne, his wife, had put together. In attendance were Doggie with his wife Jessie, Jar Head and his wife Mims, Gert, their secretary and friend at CIA, Di Flipi, and Gil Dunn.

"You kids certainly get around," Di Flipi observed then added, "Another nice job."

Blue Jay and Bean nodded their head in thanks for the kind words.

Later in the evening Bean and Blue Jay were smoking cigars on the patio when Dunn joined them.

"Those two are still going on and on about how good the French are," he relayed.

"They're pissed," Blue Jay answered.

"About what?" a surprised Dunn asked.

"They think they may have sniffed out that those people were not French and are mad because we wouldn't tell who they are," explained Bean.

"That explains why they haven't mentioned you two more," Gil said. He paused, for a few seconds then advised, "Why don't you go in and play up the it must be the training and if U.S. Intel had better instructors it would be as good as the French unit."

"Oh, that would set them free!" Blue Jay remarked.

"Let's do it," Bean suggested.

"Okay!" Blue Jay agreed and both men headed inside.

"Don't forget to work into the conversation about if your training was better," Gil again advised, "I'll count to one hundred then dial 911.

The duo laughed at Dunn's remark as they opened the patio door and headed for battle.

When the entire Team returned to the Barn from a Project, Top and the Ladies always prepared something special for the first dinner and tonight it was surf & turf, baked potato, green beans, and two big ass chocolate cakes for dessert.

There was not much talking during dinner because everyone was enjoying the delicious meal.

Top and the Ladies always enjoyed taking their meals with JJ, Mac, and the Team, especially enjoying the Bull Shit Derby that usually started after dessert.

Everyone was enjoying coffee when Pru broke the silence. "I say JJ."

"I say JJ?" Panda interrupted. "It's usually I say Top, followed by how the long guns saved the day."

"Quite so," was Pru's reply, then continued with, "I have a few questions about the Project."

"If I have the answers," JJ assured him.

Pru held a newspaper up and read the account of the rescue.

"Former CIA officials kidnapped last week by Corsican NFLC king pin were rescued today by an elite French Intelligence Unit backed by the French Foreign Legion Parachute Regiment stationed on Corsica. The Unit executed a successful daylight raid that rescued the two men while eliminating the king pin and many of his security force.

Accusation that the NFLC king pin had a financial arrangement that reached high into the French government still goes unanswered." "I am assuming the Board is responsible for all of this?"

"Maybe," JJ conceded.

"Second question," Pru continued. "How did you get the French government to agree on using their military?"

"We didn't," JJ answered, "that was just a training jump."

"But the security force thought they were coming after them," Bris remarked.

"We can't help what they thought," JJ replied.

"Okaaay," Pru said slowly. "Third question, what about the king pin having a financial arrangement that reached high into the French government?"

"That is true and has been know about for some time,' JJ assured Pru.

"But how did that help our project?" Pru asked.

"How it helped our project is not in that paper, but it was on

CNN the night they reported that unnamed sources claim French Liaison on Corsica linked to terrorist and extremely high level corruption in the French Government." JJ answered.

"You see, we had to get the liaison recalled because he was protecting SOT by sitting on the Foreign Legion. JC knew the Legion wanted to move on SOT and with the liaison out of the way the Regimental Commanding Officer was free to order a training jump in SOT's area.

"Then we followed up with giving the French all of the credit and made them heroes so they would go with the flow. The Regimental Commanding Officer will stick to his guns that it was just a training jump, but we and that Commanding Officer agree, with all of the good PR flying around, he will be persuaded to say he was supporting the Elite French Intel Unit."

"Of course that Elite French Intel Unit was this Team, but even if their Intel people try to tell them no such unit exists, the current French government won't give a shit as long as they are getting the credit. With Jar Head and Doggie heaping praise on the French and the media reporting it as fast as they can, it should last a while."

"Any other questions?" JJ inquired.

"And we thought the Board just sat around the conference table," Check said.

While things were on a serious note Blue Jay stood and announced, "Can I have your attention, would like to say something. We flipped for it and I won, so here goes."

"Bean and I want to thank all of you for your help.

Words can't express how much we appreciate it, not to mention the fact the four of us would probably be dead right now if you hadn't helped. That goes for the Board too. JJ, please convey our thanks to them as well."

JJ acknowledged he would.

"Jar Head and Doggie would be standing here thanking you as well, but as you know we had to give the Team a French Intel cover." Blue Jay continued."

"In place of them being here let me share a few things with you. As you probably already know they trained Bean and myself, but before and during that time they were very active in the Intel community and had seen and done a lot. During this Project, Jar Head and Doggie kept remarking about the good execution and organization. How we could learn a thing or two from the French and on and on. Bean and I agreed with them and I said, *'They are the best'* and Bean said, *'The very best.'"*

"I guess what I'm trying to say is Jar Head and Doggie saw you in action once and think you are very good. Bean and I know you, have been in action with you many times, and we think you are the Very Best."

Everyone at the table stayed quiet for a few seconds, which seemed like an hour, then Bean broke the silence with, "Well, it's true."

Everyone at the table laughed and expressed their appreciation for the kind words.

After another period of silence JJ inquired, "I know I'm probably going to regret this, but any stories?"

"You mean like someone sitting in an airplane, taking the pins out of grenades, then putting the grenades back into the box about one foot from your face?" Mac asked, "No, I don't know any of those types of stories."

"Did you get killed?" JC inquired, "That wasn't as bad as you bouncing bundles of lit flares around the inside of the plane. Talk about a chicken arm General."

Mac stopped laughing to correct JC. "That only happened once."

"They're good," Bean approved, "but I think what JJ has in mind is when you fight your way across a smoke and gas filled compound to an extraction point, then find out the people you're trying to save are on the second floor on an Easter egg hunt."

"You'll have to blame your Father and his obsession with those fucking hand grenades for that one," Blue Jay defended.

"Like yours doesn't have the same obsession?" Bean claimed. "I'll bet you $50 he threw one as well and another $50 that he said, *'Fuck this,'* before he pulled the pin."

Blue Jay shook his head yes and said "You're right," as he broke into laughter with Bean quickly joining him.

When they finally regrouped Blue Jay inquired, "Who were those fucking guys anyway?" He and Bean again broke into laughter this time joined by everyone at the table.

The Derby was off to another good start.

CHAPTER TEN

The Board had just started its first session since returning from Corsica.

"Are there any loose ends or questions about the last Project?" JJ inquires.

After a few seconds with no one responding Foxie asked, "Do the Projects usually include field trips for the Board?"

"No, not at all," JJ smiled. "But this wasn't the first time we went on one."

"Fair enough," Foxie replied knowing it was not going to be all boring boardroom stuff.

"Gil," JJ then inquired. "What about Jar Head and Doggie?"

"Been in touch with people at secret squirrel and they have them, their wives plus a third couple at a safe place and will help them all to relocate. Not a protected witness thing, just making it hard for any other son's that want to come out of the woodwork and avenge somebody."

"Good," JJ approved then added, "Unless there are any other issues, I guess it's back to planning the big Project."

"Admiral Fox," JJ continued. "During the first Board meeting you attended I gave you a very brief description of the current Project we are planning, but didn't get a chance to follow-up with a more detailed explanation until now. We are very small, but have a lot of resources available to us as you will see."

"We usually give the object or objects of a Project a code name then use it for everything. This is done in case someone slips up on the phone or whatever and no one will know who the person is talking about."

"For this Project we have selected Big Daddy, Bedbug and Slick."

"Big Daddy runs everything and his sons are next in line, but they are worse than Big Daddy. For general principle the entire group should be exterminated, but we have discovered a more urgent reason."

"As you know, Jeff Dawson, the President of International Oil, has spent many years in that part of the world, still having many friends and contacts in oil rich countries of the Middle East. When Jeff was coming up through the ranks he developed what he calls an Oil Intel Group. In others words, he established sources for collecting information about the oil industry in that part of the world, both friendly and unfriendly to the U.S., and has saved his company millions of dollars by getting them privy information so they can be ahead of the wave. That's probably one of the reasons he is company president today."

"It's more like the only reason in addition to I will not tell them who my contacts are," Dawson said jokingly.

"Don't let him kid you Foxie, he's a very good business man," JJ proclaimed.

"If he's running with this group, I'm sure he is," Foxie observed.

The members of the Board just looked at Foxie and smiled.

"To continue," JJ started again, "Jeff became privy to information that Big Daddy is planning something really big for his oil fields, the fields of Kuwait and Saudi Arabia. It is a simple plan if you have the right stuff, but that's where his problem lies. He's working on it, but still hasn't succeeded."

"Here's his plan by the numbers," JJ continued,

"One, he plans to develop small nuclear devices, not for missiles or aircraft bombs, just a very dirty device that can be carried by one man in a case.

Two, once the devices are developed he will send teams out into the Kuwait, Saudi and his own oil fields.

Three, to make his point and because he hates them, he will set off one of the devices in a Kuwait oil field.

Four, with that done he will make demands and threaten to set off the other devices.

Five, the world will be thrown into chaos, the people in the Middle East will think he is a hero and while other countries try to figure out what to do, he attacks Israel with missiles of all kinds.

Six, Israel will respond with nuclear missiles. Need I go on?" JJ inquired.

"No," Foxie answered, "but how do you know that's his plan?"

"Jeff, do you want to take that one?" JJ inquired.

"Sure," Dawson spoke up, "Syria Intel has infiltrated high into the ranks of Iraq's Directorate of Military Intelligence. A source at the Directorate shared it, along with their concerns about the plan, with the agent from Syria.

"Since Syria hates the West they will not inform them, but they did share it with Iran. An Iranian Intelligence Officer, who is now a very rich man, informed Kuwait of the pending disaster. My contacts in Kuwait made me aware of the situation."

"How did you verify any of this?" Foxie asked.

"Over to you, Gil" Dawson requested.

"When Dawson presented this at one of our meetings we decided it was too dangerous not to check out," Dunn started, "First, Jeff instructed his Oil Intel group to pull out all of the stops in finding out any additional information about the topic. I made personal contacts with CIA people I know can be trusted, told them the story, and asked them to look into the matter."

"When all of our sources reported back we had a shit load of information and decided to leak it all to the administration. That went well to a point. They agreed there was a nuclear effort underway, but somebody up there they all listened to, insisted it was to develop missile warheads only."

"And that's where we are right now," JJ again took control of the meeting, "If we do nothing one of two things will happen. Big Daddy will execute his plan or eventually the U.S. will declare war on Iraq."

"The one that worries me the most is Big Daddy executing his plan," Foxie said with concern. "If all of those things you outlined happen, the Middle East will go up, but what about those countries that depend on Middle East oil more than we do? They may side with Iraq to keep their oil flowing and save their economies. Before we can help countries with technology and drilling to replace the oil they require, World War Three could break out."

"Exactly," JJ confirmed. "We really don't want to take on this Project, but feel we have to do something."

"The Team has the right to turn down any Project, but are in total agreement with the Board."

"Now that you are really caught up to date," JJ continued, "you can join us in some decision making."

"We will be able to take out Big Daddy and one of his sons if all goes well with the Project. The question is which one, Bedbug or Slick? I guess the question boils down to which one is more dangerous and should be eliminated? We have voted three and three after each discussion on the subject, so I guess you will be the tie breaker."

"I'll give you my honest opinion on the subject," Foxie assured the Board.

"Fair enough," JJ said as he started yet another discussion on which son should go with Big Daddy."

After two hours of discussion, the Board members had exhausted all of their reasons on why Bedbug or Slick should be eliminated.

"I think everyone has expressed their views on the matter," JJ observed, "Shall we vote?"

The Board members all agreed.

"To take the mystery out of it, we'll ask Foxie for his vote first," JJ announced.

Foxie sat up and moved closer to the conference table. "All of the reasons on both sides of the question are valid," he started, "but my primary concern is which son would be more likely to follow through with his father's plan with the nuclear devices? The answer is probably both, but I feel Bedbug, more so then Slick, would carry out the plan. So my vote is Bedbug."

"Good point," JJ approved. "I was thinking more along the lines of Slick being head of the Intelligence and other agencies being more dangerous. I figured Bedbug would probably go into a crazy fit that no one would pay any attention to him since his father was gone."

"If we could count on that or Bedbug trying to lay claim to the throne and cause a riff between himself and his followers on one side, and the generals, the party in power, on the other, I would say Slick also," Dunn admitted, "But Bedbug is totally insane and with Big Daddy out of the picture and no one else able to control him he is capable of anything."

"Unless someone else has something to add I'll consider the matter closed," JJ conceded.

When no one offered any additional comments, JJ announced, "I'll call a Team meeting tomorrow and forward the decision along with all of the reasons."

"Now that we have that resolved are there any other outstanding problems connected with the next Project?" JJ asks.

"I believe Dawson and Dunn were having a 'who can you trust in Kuwait' discussion the last time we were meeting about this Project,'" Mac offered.

"That is correct," JJ said as he patted Mac on his right shoulder. "Has that issue been resolved?" he inquired.

"I regret to inform you the answer is a capital NO ," Dawson informed JJ.

"I was afraid you were going to say something like that,"

JJ replied. "Okay, sound the bell to start the next round," he instructed and motioned toward Dawson to continue.

CHAPTER ELEVEN

The language classes were back in session and Check was giving special tutoring to Bris and Tic who would require better understanding and speaking skills if they were challenged during the second phase of the Project.

JC was running Air Jockey through time trials on the ID gizmo. Jockey would be required to confirm within a few seconds the target was Big Daddy and not a look-alike. JC was filling in as the target and was located approximately 800 yards away going through different movements while Jockey tried to get a fix on him for ID purposes. Once the ID was fed into a powerful laptop PC, the ID match or mismatch took only seconds.

"Is it soup yet?" JC inquired over the com unit he and Jockey were using.

"You're moving around too fast," Jockey accused.

"Well, under the circumstances, the subject will probably be moving around fast," JC fired back, "Pick up the cadence."

"Pick up this," Jockey muttered, as he finally got a fix on JC and fired it into the PC.

"Got it," Jockey confirmed, as the PC displayed positive ID.

"Well that's good," JC approved, "now all we have to do is to get Big Daddy to show up a little early and move a little slower that day."

"Instead of using this spotter scope, it would help if we had it hooked into the scope on a rifle," Jockey offered. "Preferably a rifle with a live round in the chamber and the safety off, but I promise to be careful. Unfortunately, accidents do happen during training." Jockey was waiting for a reply, but the com unit stayed quiet. After a few seconds Jockey looked through the spotter scope and saw JC just standing there. "You all right?" Jockey inquired.

"Yes," JC assured Jockey, "and give the man from Pussy Airways a cigar."

"Okay," Jockey agreed not knowing why.

"Meet you in the com shack," JC announced as he started to return to the Barn.

JC picked up Blue Jay on the way and all three men were in the com shack when JC announced, "Out of the mouths of babes. Jockey came up with a good idea."

"The way we've been training," JC explained, "using a scope, Jockey has been trying to get a fix on me and then feeding it into the PC for a match. If I move too fast or he has a bad angle it takes too long."

"Here is his idea," JC continued. "We hook the PC directly into the scope on a rifle or attach the PC scope that feeds the image directly into the PC for ID. This leaves Jockey free to work only with the PC to confirm the target. Bean will keep the target in the scope and send more images to the PC if needed. It should speed up sending the image to the PC and getting a yes or no confirmation."

"Sounds good," Blue Jay approved, "I'll go get Bean and we'll run it past him since he will be the one spotting for me."

"Good job," Blue Jay congratulated Jockey as he started to leave the com shack.

"Not bad for a man from Pussy Airways," Jockey offered.

"Not bad at all," Blue Jay approved.

"You pecker head," JC said in a low voice, "I should have told him the truth about how you were planning the assassination of your beloved team leader."

"JC, Bubbie," Jockey pleaded. "You know I was just kidding. Here have a cigar. I know smoking these things aren't good for us, but somebody has to do it."

"I can't remember who the ass wipe was that got me started on this filthy habit. Wait a minute, it was you!" Jockey faked a moment of realization.

"Ass wipe, eh? I'm telling about your assassination plan," JC threatened and said in a low voice, "Oh Mr. JJ."

That remark caused Jockey to laugh out loud followed by their usual war of words until Blue Jay returned with Bean.

Bean agreed with the idea and offered a few ideas on how to attach the PC scope to a rifle, then said, "If you didn't make us throw those .308 Remington light weights away, we could have used one of them."

"You mean those .308 Remington light weights we gave to the Cuban Freedom Fighters for helping the Team, don't you?"

Blue Jay inquired, then added, "and I still say, 'Fuck a mine field.'"

"You're both wrong. That story has been updated," JC corrected, "Now it's, those .308 Remington light weights we gave to Charley Tuna, the Cuban mobster, for helping the Team."

"We stand corrected," both men agreed with a chuckle.

After a brief silence Bean wondered out loud,

"I don't know which you dislike more, mine fields or authority."

"I dislike mine fields, authority, and especially you,"

Blue Jay answered.

"Like I give a fuck, he who shits through feathers," Bean fired back.

"Oh yeah," Blue Jay said. "Well beans usually just make me fart, but you make me shit."

"You know, I'll bet we could secure a small bar along the bottom of the PC scope," Bean started.

"And attach rifle clamps that could use the grooves already on the rifle," Blue Jay finished.

Air Jockey looked at JC, smiled and shook his head at the duo.

"What?" JC questioned Jockey. "Didn't you people over at Pussy Airways solve problems this way?"

"I guess it's their turn," Bean said and Blue Jay agreed with a head shake as they continued analyzing the problem.

With most of the Team planning completed and technical problems resolved, it was time to kick the Team's physical fitness up a notch.

JC had posted the first weekly 'Lock On Training Schedule' and Panda had made his usual "Lock on This" comment, signaling the official start of the Team's moving from very good physical condition to excellent.

This time Lock On would include a one-week road trip to Death Valley for day and night training.

The Board had completed their planning and making of arrangements, with the exception of the Dawson/Dunn debate.

To resolve their deadlock they had agreed to put the source to a test. If he passed it was a go, if he didn't there would be a short delay. Dunn's only concern was the safety of the Team. He knew the source could be trusted when it came to passing information and other things, but a Team of men?

Safeguards were also being put into place to help ensure the source stayed on the level.

CHAPTER TWELVE

One month had passed since Lock On Training started and the Team had returned from their road trip.

Everyone had their picture taken for their new forged ID's. Between the new black uniforms they were all trying on for size, and the training at Death Valley, they all looked like homeies from that part of the world.

A Team meeting had been called to review the Project and especially the how's. How do we get in, How do we get it done, and How in the hell do we get out?

The team had been a little skeptical of the in and out part since planning started and they were discussing it again. During a brief silence Pru spoke up, "I say, does anyone mind if I cast in my two cents about this dictator?"

"Dictater? Isn't that what you get when you cross a penis with a potato?" asked Panda.

"Quit so," replied Pru, then continued, "We all realize this is a brutal dictatorship and I would like to draw some comparisons and a little history from another dictatorship, Nazi Germany."

"No offence intended, Met old boy," Pru assured.

"Don't worry about me," Met replied, "I'm still trying to figure out the penis and the potato thing."

"History has told us of how spies and the underground sometimes used the fear of the SS and the Gestapo to complete their operations." Pru continued, "I feel we have a similar situation where we are going and with that goes the fear for his special units and personal guard."

"If we are to use that fear successfully, we must have no doubts about the parts we are playing. That's how they got it done in World War Two; act like a big ass SS officer and everyone would usually give into fear."

"My grandfather told me a story about the fear factor that may help. This chap from British Intel was sent with the Belgium Underground to get copies of the German searchlight plans for the coast prior to D-Day. Reason being, where there are searchlights there are is usually anti-aircraft guns protecting something."

"The group had no problem getting into the office and finding the map, but at that point the plan took two paths. The Brit was setting up his photo gear to take a picture of the map and the underground leader was rolling up the map. 'I have to get a picture of it' says the Brit. 'We are taking it with us, says the underground leader.' 'But they will know,' the Brit confirmed. 'Let me tell you how it will go,' the leader started. 'If they do realize it is gone, one of two things will happen. When they bring it to the General's attention, he will say it was destroyed and make up the documents to show when they burned it or they will blame a private and shoot him before anyone can find out the truth.'

'The reason, the leader continued,' Hitler hates almost all of the generals and thinks they are out to get him, so none of them are going to give him a reason to put them against a wall.' 'But we can't be sure,' the Brit pleaded. 'I don't know what you are going to do, but we're leaving and we're taking the map with us,' the leader informed the Brit as he continued rolling up the map."

"They took the map, everyone got home safe, and the missing map problem never saw the light of day."

"I guess the bottom line is the Belgiums knew a weakness in their enemy, believed it, and used it."

"Another weakness was the fear of special units close to the Dictator. The Belgium and underground resistance from other countries would sometimes impersonate SS and Gestapo units to execute their operations.

"Can this Dictator be less brutal than Hitler? Worse I'd say. Even the army is afraid of his special units, just like the German Army was afraid of the SS in Nazi Germany."

"If we are challenged during the in and out phase, Check, acting as our commanding officer, will bully his way through the situation with the rest of us backing his play in a threatening manner."

"So you're saying, when in Rome, do as the Romans do?" Met offered.

"More like, do as the Belgium's do, actually," Pru corrected. "What if we run into a real unit from this personal guard that can't be bullied?" Tic inquired.

"The personal guard is usually kept inside the city so we shouldn't have any problems before that," Blue Jay answered, "but if we do run into them, it may be lock and load time."

"The reasoning is sound and history does repeat itself," Benz offered, "Let's just hope those assholes haven't been watching things about World War Two on the History Channel."

The Team members agreed with Benz and laughed at his History Channel remark.

Having agreed on the main topic, other items were addressed like the special gizmos.

The meeting went on for several more hours, sometimes covering an item for more times than anyone could count, but when the meeting was over, all of the planning and training had been completed.

As the meeting came to a close, JC looked at his watch and declared, "Chow time," signaling it was time for dinner.

When the Team members were seated around the big dining room table, they were joined by JJ and Mac.

Top and the Ladies served everyone before being seated at the table themselves.

During dinner the conversation was light and humorous as usual, but during coffee it got a little more serious when questions were asked about the upcoming Project.

Several questions had been asked and answered when Top made an inquiry, "Who is going to watch home base in Kuwait?"

"That will be JC, Mac, and myself," JJ replied.

"According to the plan that will leave only one at home base for some hours during Team insertion and extraction," LadyA offered.

"That's true," JJ answered, "but it should only be a matter of hours."

"I'm wondering if three people are enough to secure home base in that part of the world?" Lady1 asked.

JJ was wondering why these questions were being asked, but JC and the Team could already see where this conversation was going and had big smiles on their faces as they toyed with their coffee cups.

"That is also true," JJ replied, "but it can't be helped."

"Not necessarily," Top contradicted.

"What do you mean?" JJ asked with a puzzled look on his face.

"Well, the Ladies and I were discussing it," Top started to explain, but was cut off in mid sentence.

"Oh no, not again," JJ ordered "When you all joined us for the emergency D.C. Project it bothered me very much, but at least the Ladies were inside the U.S.. This time we will be in a foreign country and in the Middle East at that."

"We used to do that sort of thing for a living or have you forgotten?" Lady1 inquired.

"No I haven't forgotten," JJ replied, "but field work is not what you have signed on for."

"Sounds like discrimination to me," LadyA announced, "Maybe a law suit is in order."

"I'll bet that would make it into big time media," Panda announced.

"I can see it all now," Air Jockey added, "Two women, code-named Lady1 and LadyA, bring discrimination suit against JJ and," "Do we have an official name?" Jockey stopped to inquire.

"No, but a few names are coming to mind," JJ answered.

"Brings discrimination suit against JJ and the secret team," Jockey started again. "Ladies claim they were not allowed to go on secret mission even though they had their stilettos sharpened up and had learned to say, 'Carry out' in several Middle East lingos."

"Don't bring that up again," Panda pleaded, "still remember how they scared that gang in D.C. and how they threatened them. I still can't eat bratwurst."

"Do you have any control over this herd," JJ inquired to JC.

"Sometimes," JC replied. "Why don't we hear what the Ladies and Top have in mind?"

"I'll listen," JJ agreed, "but I'm not promising anything."

JJ, Mac, and the Team sat back and listened as the three

presented their case. Their involvement would require little or no changes in the original plan, would help to secure home base and their ride back to Jersey.

Top and the Ladies made a valid argument and with some help from the Team persuaded JJ to change his mind.

CHAPTER THIRTEEN

It was day one of the Project and everyone had assembled outside the Barn. All of the weapons and technical gizmos had been loaded into the special hidden compartments of the panel truck that Mac and JC would be driving to the airport.

The team were wearing jeans and shirts like they were going to a casual event, but the inside of their cloth suitcases told another story. There were camouflage utilities, black suits, and scarves inside. The usual weekend getaway bag.

Top and the Ladies were also in casual dress with their suitcase contents similar to the Team members.

JC surveyed the group and inquired, "Are we ready?"

"Let's do it," was the group reply as the Team members headed for the three vans that would be transporting them to the airport.

The vehicles would leave the Barn at one minute intervals to avoid the look of a convoy. JJ would be in the first van and would alert the others if any problems occurred on the way to Mercer Airport. JC and Mac in the truck will be second followed by the other two vans.

Each vehicle followed the dirt road that led to Route 29. Once they had reached that road, they paused for a few seconds waiting for other cars or trucks to pass that would put a space between their vehicles.

Knowing the traffic light in Lambertville would probably cause the group to bunch up, they took different streets. JJ passed through town before the others.

JC and Mac in the truck stayed on Main street, passed Cifelli's Sunoco and continued south on route 29. The van behind the truck turned left at York Street, then right onto Franklin. After passing Mason's Bar they proceeded onto route 179 and seconds later were back on route 29.

The remaining van also stayed on Route 29, but kept some distance from the truck. By the time JC and Mac passed the River

Walk office complex the vans were back in position.

At this point Route 29 was four lanes until it reached the Lambertville City limits, then it went back into two lanes. The truck and the two vans took advantage of the other cars needing to get to the city limits first even though they would be in the same position for about the next ten miles. When they continued down Route 29 the group had about one or two cars between them and settled in for a slow ride to the airport. As Mac and JC passed through Washington Crossing, Mac's thoughts again reflected back to those brave men that crossed the Delaware River with General Washington, marched to Trenton and won a battle that saved the American Revolution. Brave hearts all.

When the first van arrived at Mercer Field, JJ continued to the private hangar where the jet was waiting.

Upon arrival he spoke with the chief maintenance mechanic to get the status of the plane. When he was satisfied everything was ready he inquired if they had seen his pilot. When they all said no, JJ said a few unkind words about the pilot, then informed the crew they could have the rest of the day off, handed the chief mechanic a $50 bill and told him to take his crew to breakfast.

After the men had departed for breakfast, the truck and vans approached the jet, quickly loaded their gear and all of the goodies in the truck onto the plane.

The suitcases would have been okay, but loading weapons may have caused a few questions from the mechanics.

While the plane was being loaded, Air Jockey was in the jet's cockpit with JC quickly going through the checklist.

"Slow down," JC requested, "what's your hurry?"

"The New Jersey State Police Aviation Bureau is right across the field," Jockey replied.

"So?" JC inquired.

"So," Jockey quipped, "I had a dream last night that three of their Bell helicopters were over here hovering and announcing over their speaker system, 'Everyone deplane and stand away from the jet.'"

JC looked up from the checklist and stated, "The man from PAW," then returned to the list.

"PAW?" Jockey questioned.

"Yeah," JC replied, "Pussy Air Ways."

"Oh that's funny," Jockey commented, trying not to laugh at the one-liner.

When Jockey regrouped he questioned, "Will we be seeing a repeat performance of the landing in Mexico or will you be doing that extra little bit more and just crash the fucking plane."

JC didn't look up from the checklist, but smiled as he said, "The man from PAW."

Fifteen minutes and a half-dozen one-liners later, the jet had just received permission for take-off.

The jet rolled down the runway until it reached take-off speed and Jockey pulled it into the air. JC was looking out the side window during take off then announced, "Guess we're safe. I don't see any fighter planes down there with NJSP on the side."

"So it's going to be one of those kind of flights is it?" Jockey inquired then yelled to the others, "Panda, who's in the lead for the Annual JC Crazy Fuck Award?"

"Blue Jay," Panda confirmed, "But I have a bad feeling the person the award is named after wants the title back."

"You mean JC?" Jockey asked.

"I'm not mentioning any names," Panda declined.

"Another one, JC announced, "The man from PAP, Pussy Air Philippines."

"Don't smear his name around like that," LadyA pleaded.

Complete silence filled the plane as everyone looked at LadyA.

Seeing she was the center of attention she explained, "Get it, PAP Smear," she explained.

"Yeah, we got it," the Team agreed as they all broke into laughter.

"She knows one when she sees one," JC confirmed.

"This usually happens after the Project is completed," JJ said to Mac.

"Wonder what the trip back is going to be like?" Mac replied.

———————

After a stop for fuel the jet continued on to Kuwait.

The plan was for the Oil Intel group to have a cargo plane with Iranian markings ready to go and to keep the area secure until they were contacted by radio to leave the area.

When their jet was about an hour from landing at the field, JC made contact with the Intel group, thanked them and told they could depart.

Sixty minutes later the jet was making a slow pass over a remote airstrip. A pair of eyes were in every window of the plane looking for any signs of personnel or anything out of the ordinary. After a second pass the jet circled around the field, came in for a landing, and taxied up close to a small hanger that was in serious disrepair.

Wearing a dust mask to conceal his identity, JC quickly deplaned, and moved out in front to help guide the jet. Giving Jockey hand signals he brought the plane forward until the plane was inside the hangar, then signaled a halt. With the exception of where the plane entered there were no openings for prying eyes from the outside and as the jet engines wined down to a halt, JC moved quickly to close that opening. When he got to the rear of the jet and surveyed the hangar doors, he saw they were inoperative, but the Oil Intel group had jury rigged a series of rolled up canvas held in place by ropes tied off at separate sides of the opening. After quickly checking for any signs of booby traps, JC untied one of the ropes and slowly lowered the first canvas. That done he went to the next one and continued until all were down, completely blocking the entrance.

When the door of the plane again opened JJ, Mac, Top, and the Team quickly got off with suitcases in hand and started to change. Blue Jay had JC's suitcase in tow and they joined the others as they all changed into their camies. The Ladies remained on the jet and were doing the same.

After the Team members got changed, they proceeded with their assigned duties.

Benz and Panda, after getting their spotter scopes, proceeded to opposite ends of the hangar and started to scan the area. If anyone was out there, the area facing the once opened end of the hangar would be the smart place to be, so Benz took special care when scanning.

Pru and Met retrieved the drag bags containing the .50 caliber rifles, took out the rifle scopes, and proceeded to opposite sides of the hangar to find or create an opening and started to scan those areas.

That completed, Pru and Met returned to the drag bags and started to assemble the .50s as Panda joined Benz. When the rifles were assembled Met and Pru took up positions on opposite sides of the hangar entrance with Panda and Benz taking up spotter positions. The canvases were put to good use as the shooters and spotters were concealed from view with only their scopes and the barrels of the .50s protruding through openings between the unrolled canvases. With spotters and shooters in place JC, Air Jockey, Bris, Tic, and Check put on their dust masks and proceeded to the cargo plane to start checking it out. In order not to give away the total number in the group, everyone else would stay inside the hangar.

When the five men got to the plane they immediately checked for booby traps around the plane. Then JC checked the side door and slowly opened it. Once the door was opened the five entered and continued checking. Jockey moved slowly to the plane's cockpit and checked for anything unusual.

When all were satisfied JC turned on one of his gizmos and started scanning the plane for bugs and homing devices. Tic joined Jockey to help with the checklist while Bris and Check went back outside to check the fuel and tires for tampering.

The shooters and spotters were watching for any unwanted visitors and especially for the sun flashing off of binoculars or rifle scopes.

"Flash at 10 o'clock," Benz alerted into his com unit and all attention focused on that area.

"Got him," Panda relayed to the others, "He's about 1,000 yards out with a pair of binoculars."

"Acquired," Met confirmed, letting everyone know he could take the subject out.

"See any others," JC inquired? "not yet," Benz replied, as he and Pru continued to scan the area while Panda and Met kept in touch with the subject.

"Maybe some movement at 11 o'clock, but it's hard to tell with these thermal ripples in the air," Benz announced.

"We're almost done here," JC informed everyone, "Will rejoin you soon." Which meant, keep those assholes under surveillance until we get back to the hangar.

Blue Jay and Bean had joined the search and were checking out other directions for movement of any kind.

Ten minutes had passed when JC and the others returned and everyone gathered at the front of the hangar.

JC first borrowed Panda's spotter scope to check out the situation. While he was doing so, Benz reported no other activity sighted, followed by the same report from Bean and Blue Jay about the others areas around the hangar.

"Well, it's either somebody from that Oil Intel group spying on us or some bad people sizing us up?" JC reported as he returned the spotter scope to Panda.

"Break out the night vision gear," he instructed, "It'll be dark soon and if they don't make a move we'll go snoopin and poopin to see who they are."

Three hours of darkness had passed with Blue Jay and Check just returning from a recon patrol.

"Anything?" JC inquired.

"Looks like bandits on a day trip from Iraq," Blue Jay reported."

"I think they were close enough to see the jet landing and decided to check things out," Check added.

"Think they'll move on us?" JC inquired.

"Afraid so," Check confirmed, "but they are debating on tonight or first light."

"How many?" JC asked.

"Ten with three jeeps." Check confirmed.

"The Team will grab some sack time while the rest of us keep watch with the night vision gear," JC announced without hesitation. "We'll run two-hour shifts. The Ladies and myself will take the first shift and in two hours be relieved by JJ, Mac, and Top.

"Any questions?" No questions were asked and everyone turned to.

———————

It was about an hour before dawn would break and no activity had been spotted.

"I guess they've either changed their minds or we'll be having visitors soon," JC said to LadyA and Lady1.

As the three continued their watch they thought they smelled freshly brewed coffee, but didn't believe it. The Team was also picking up on the fragrance and was starting to stir from their sleep. JC started looking for the source of the smell and as he came around the back of the jet, he discovered Top brewing two large pots of coffee. "I don't believe it!" JC exclaimed.

"Well, one has to be civilized even in the field," Top explained.

"Quite so," Pru approved as he arrived with his canteen cup in hand.

Top looked at Pru and both broke into laughter.

"Everyone up," JC ordered, "it's time to be civilized."

When JC rejoined the Ladies he told them to go grab some coffee while he kept watch.

Five minutes later Blue Jay was standing beside JC with some coffee in two canteen cups.

"Think they'll come?" Blue Jay asked.

"Have a feeling they will," JC replied as he accepted the coffee.

"How do you want to handle it?" Blue Jay inquired.

"We have to keep them away from both planes for starters," JC answered.

An hour passed and three jeeps were heading in the direction of the hangar. When the jeeps were within two hundred yards, JC pushed the canvas aside, walked out, moved to his right away from the hangar and the jet inside.

The lead jeep saw JC, changed course and headed directly for him. JC didn't speak the language, but Check would be on the com unit translating if the leader didn't speak English.

The jeeps stopped about ten yards from JC and everyone except the leader dismounted with guns at the ready. Half were watching JC and the other half the hangar.

"What are you doing here? This is my place," the leader inquired in broken English.

"I don't think so," JC answered.

"Are you calling me a liar?" the leader asked.

"No, I just don't think this place is yours," JC replied as he moved a little to the left, per request from Panda on the com unit, and at the same time resting his hand on the 9mm in his holster.

"You American dog," the leader erupted, as he produced a long knife. "I'll cut off your head, but first I'll skin you."

"Skin this mother fucker," JC commanded as he drew his 9mm and fired while saying, "Do it" into the com unit.

Between eighteen to twenty rounds were fired by the Team, then there was silence as nine bandits fell to the ground. The leader was still sitting in his jeep, holding his knife, and sporting a new third eye between the other two.

The Team quickly moved out of the hangar to check the fallen bandits.

"Break the vehicles out of the plane!" JC barked, "And load these men into their jeeps. We have to dump them a good distance from here."

Check, Tic, and Bris went to the plane and a few minutes later the back ramp was being lowered. When it was touching the ground, one then another Iraqi vehicle was driven down the ramp.

The bodies had been loaded into the bandits' jeeps with Blue Jay, Bean and Panda sitting behind the wheels of the jeeps. As the Iraqi vehicles approached the jeeps Blue Jay took the lead for the garbage detail.

Several miles from the airstrip he found a reasonably concealed area. He pulled into the area, stopped and the other two jeeps pulled alongside him. The six men did their best with what was available to conceal the three jeeps, then departed.

When they returned everyone except the drivers got out of the Iraqi vehicles and they were again backed into the plane.

Benz and the shooters had been scanning the area for any other bad people that might have been in the area while Top and the Ladies policed up the empty shell casings. There were nineteen 9mm casings from JC and the Team, but only a few from the others. However, one of the bandit rounds came close to getting lucky when it passed through JC's left sleeve.

JC called everyone into the hangar while Mac and JJ scanned the area for any other intruders.

As the last of the group were arriving, Panda motioned to the hole in JC's sleeve and said, "I knew you couldn't stand being out of first place."

JC looked at his sleeve then announced, "I liked it better in this part of the world when the most trouble you could get into was a camel shit fight with a bunch of nomads."

The group burst into laughter partly for the one liner, but mostly for the serious delivery.

When the laughter subsided, JC started talking seriously. "We are still on schedule and the Team will be departing at 1300 hours. The security around the hangar will have to be especially tight. We have night scopes, rifles, and automatic weapons to repel any unwanted visitors."

"Any questions?" he asked. When no one spoke up JC added, "Just one more thing. So there will not be any problems in the chain of command, we gave Mac only one round and told him to use it on himself if anything serious happened to the high command."

As everyone chuckled, Bean whispered to Blue Jay, "where have I heard that line before?"

"That line does get around," he replied.

Mac was caught off guard, but was quick to recover and fired a volley back at JC as the group dispersed .

For the Team, weapons cleaning and a little sack time would be the order of the day until take off.

CHAPTER FOURTEEN

At 1300 hours the cargo plane was taxiing out to the strip for take off and at 1310 it was at take off speed, as JC pulled back on the controls and the plane glided into the air. The plane left Kuwait and headed out over the Persian Gulf. Fifteen minutes into the flight the plane dropped down low as if it was making a landing at another part of Kuwait, then banked left and headed for the Iranian coast. Due to the no-fly zones, if they used Iraqi airspace in the South or North, they would be challenged by U.S. fighters and forced to land.

JC and Air Jockey would guide the aircraft along the Zagron Mountain Range until they were parallel with Bagdad then move in closer to the Iraqi border.

Several hours into the flight Jockey announced, "It's time to make a left."

"Looks that way," JC confirmed as he slowly banked the plane to the left.

"I hope those Oil Intel people have it right about a dirt road where we want to land," JC wondered out loud.

"It's rough ass country," Jockey agreed.

A short time later Air Jockey informed JC, "We should be coming up on the landing location very soon."

"All I see is the tops of small mountains," JC replied as he and Jockey scanned the area below.

"Oh this is good," Jockey started, "I see a dirt road at 3 o'clock, but it's in the middle of two small mountains."

JC banked the plane a little to the right, then back to the left so he could get a better look at the road.

"I hope this is not as good as it gets," JC observed.

"According to the coordinates they gave us we are very close."

JC and Jockey kept looking then were surprised when the road led them into a small valley that was almost hidden from view.

"It isn't much, but its home," Jockey observed.

"Let's take a look," JC said as he started a gentle left turn at the same time dropping to a lower altitude.

After circling the area JC observed, "It looks like the road is the only option. That terrain is too rough even for this aircraft."

"I'll say," Jockey agreed.

"Think I'll bring it in from east to west," JC advised.

"Works for me," Jockey approved.

The plane made a long lumbering turn to get on final approach. JC was flying so low you could almost touch the mountain peaks. When the road entered the small valley, JC started a steep descent then leveled off as he brought the big bird in for a landing. Seconds later the plane was making a very gentle landing on the dirt road.

"Nice job," Jockey congratulated JC as the plane rolled to a stop.

"Getting out is going to be interesting," JC confided to Jockey. "I'm glad we wouldn't have those vehicles onboard."

"I wonder if Mac will still enjoy the plane rides after this one?" Jockey asked with a smile.

"Let's go see how he's doing," JC suggested.

As Jockey and JC entered the back area of the plane they could hear Mac saying, "I don't know what you children want; that landing was pretty good."

"He was just behaving because you were onboard," Panda advised.

The Team was un-securing the three vehicles as Blue Jay lowered the rear ramp. When ready Check, Tic, and Bris got behind the wheels of the three vehicles and slowly drove them off the plane followed by the Team.

When everyone was outside they looked around as they loaded a few additional things onto the vehicles.

"Holy shit," Panda exclaimed. "How did he manage to land here? In Mexico he had a whole desert and he landed like he wanted to crash."

"Don't listen to them, Mac. The Mexico landing was smoother than this one," JC announced.

Panda couldn't believe his ears, then offered, "Yeah, that's right, Mac. I confess, we're all pussies."

"See, I told you, Mac," JC added, then said, "I want to see all of you kids at the post-project Bull Shit Derby, so don't take any unnecessary chances."

"That's right," Mac added, "if it comes to you children getting back or completing the Project, Fuck the Project."

"Jockey," JC called, "want to go down the road and set up an approximate point of no return for take off?"

"Will do," Jockey answered from the lead vehicle then added, "Good luck." And the entire Team echoed his words.

"Thank you," JC replied before saying, "If I was by myself I wouldn't need it, but since I have fat ass with me for the return trip..."

"Fat ass!" Mac snapped, "Why you pecker head! I still can't figure out how you got past Captain."

"Yeah, yeah, yeah," JC replied as he pushed the handle to close the ramp.

"It's not going to be quiet on the return trip," Blue Jay commented as he motioned for Bean to move out.

As the three vehicles moved to setup a point of no return, JC taxied the plane in the other direction to get as much distance as he could for take off.

When JC was in position for take off, he stood on the brake and revved up all four engines. When they were singing he released the brake and the aircraft leapt forward and started down the road. The plane was picking up speed, but not enough for take off yet.

"Not enough speed," JC told Mac. "Do you want me to abort and take another shot?"

"Put the pedal to the metal," Mac answered.

"No problem," JC replied.

"It's going to be close," Jockey informed the Team as the plane approached their position.

JC and Mac blew past the vehicles and it was a make or break situation.

JC was finally able to get the plane into the air, but would not be able to clear the small mountain at the end of the valley.

"Come on, get it higher," Panda says out loud as the Team

107

wondered if JC and Mac were going to make it.

The plane was heading straight for rocky cliffs when JC made a maneuver you usually saw performed by a fighter plane. Using air brakes and every other trick he knew, JC banked the plane so hard to the right the cargo plane was almost sideways as it made the turn. It was very close, but they made it. JC made a pass over the Team before departing, dipping the wings from side to side as he flew over them.

"That's our JC," Panda proclaimed, "He really wants to keep the title."

"Nothing like starting a project on an adrenaline rush," Jockey exclaimed.

"Let's load up," Blue Jay ordered and the Team members got back into the Iraqi vehicles for the trip to Baghdad.

———————

The members of each vehicle were broken down by shooter, spotter, and driver.

In the third vehicle would be Met and Panda with Bris driving.

The second vehicle had Pru and Benz with Tic behind the wheel.

Blue Jay, Bean, and Check, with the addition of Air Jockey who would man the ID gizmo, will be in the lead vehicle.

Since Check spoke the language fluently and looked the part, he would be acting as leader of the entire group. Bean was behind the wheel because he could speak the lingo better than the other two.

The vehicles headed back down the valley road toward the mission. The first objective was to get across the Iraqi border before they were intercepted by an Iranian patrol.

Blue Jay was busy with maps, the global positioning device, and instructing Bean on direction changes from time to time to avoid any known settlements.

It was 2200 hours(10 P.M.) when the Team reached the Iraqi border and Blue Jay called a halt.

Since they were already wearing night vision gear they sat,

looked and listened. Gil Dunn supplied them with information about where to cross. Apparently, CIA had known for quite some time that Iraqi Intel used this and a few other areas from time to time to jump the border into Iran.

Ten minutes had passed and Check had been scanning the border crossing with a listening device trying to detect noise of any kind, but not a sound could be heard.

Suddenly the sound of a vehicle approaching from the Iranian side of the border could be heard. As it crossed over the border it was challenged by several armed Iraqis and Check focused the listening device on the stopped vehicle and tried to pickup the conversation.

"What's the scoop?" Blue Jay inquired.

"Seems like that vehicle is returning from an Intel mission and the people that stopped them are people they left there to secure the crossing," Check reported then added, "The security detachment is reporting they heard vehicles in the area about ten minutes ago."

"A man in the challenged vehicle suggests it may be an Iranian border patrol or someone trying to jump the border into Iraq and wants them to stay in position until daybreak."

"Fuck that," Blue Jay commented, "let's mount up."

Since everyone is wearing com gear they heard everything Check said, plus Blue Jay could explain the plan as they were on the move.

"We can't wait until daybreak, so we have to drive these assholes off the crossing. Spread out the vehicles, pretend we are a border patrol, and charge the crossing. When I give the word everyone start firing their automatic weapons. We want a lot of noise more then anything. If they run we'll pretend to give chase into Iraq. If they make a stand we'll flush their toilet."

As Blue Jay was talking the vehicles were moving into position as they moved toward the crossing.

The border conversation was still going on when Blue Jay instructed Check to yell something to generate a little fear into them.

Check stood up in the vehicle and yelled something at the top of his lungs. When he had completed his message, Blue Jay told everyone to fire and seven automatic weapons open fire on the crossing area.

Between the message and rounds flying around them, the security detachment members jumped into the stopped vehicle as it started to flee the area.

"Keep on them!" Blue Jay instructed as they approached the border crossing.

The three vehicles crossed the border and anyone observing the incident would think they were an over eager border patrol chasing Iraqi's back home.

"Cease fire and get into line!" Blue Jay instructed, "We'll slow down and follow these people for a while to give them a big lead then we'll disappear."

When the chase took the Team over its first hill, Blue Jay spoke into the com unit. "We are going to slow down and make a U-turn back toward the hill we just came over."

The column slowed to a speed that would enable them to make a U-turn then the lead vehicle made the turn followed by the other three.

As they were moving slowly back toward the hill Blue Jay was again on the com. "When I call the driver's name, kill your lights, get off the gas, and let the vehicles roll to a stop without breaking."

He then said, "Bean," and the lights on the first vehicle went out. After Tic, then Bris' name was called the column rolled to a halt.

From the Iraqi side it looked like the patrol gave up the chase and one by one went back over that hill and out of sight. On the Iranian side, it appeared the border patrol was giving chase back to Baghdad.

"Let's get Iraqi," Blue Jay ordered and everyone dismounted, opened their packs, and broke out their black Fedayeen suits complete with matching scarves.

As they changed Blue Jay inquired, "What did you yell at those turds anyway?"

"I said, Get those Iraqi dogs, we'll cut off their balls and hang them in the square," Check answered.

"I thought they seemed eager to leave the area,"
Blue Jay mused.

Blue Jay finished consulting his map and GPD then said, "We'll make another U-turn and about a mile down this road we'll turn onto another one that shoots off to the right. For about the next five miles no vehicle lights, we'll just use the night vision gear and try to stay off the brakes." Everyone acknowledged and they moved out.

The Team kept moving until they were on the outskirts of Baghdad, then held up. They wanted to enter the city after dark. Not too early and not too late, but when the city was starting to mellow out after a busy day.

CHAPTER FIFTEEN

It was getting late in the afternoon when Blue Jay again reviewed this part of the plan. They would stay in constant communications, but from different locations.

It might have seemed like overkill, but Blue Jay wanted everyone to be crystal clear about this part of the plan. If a mistake was made, it would probably be the end of the Project and the Team.

When the review was completed Blue Jay asked if there were any questions.

"I'm clear about the plan," Panda said, "but how do we know Big Daddy will show up?"

Blue Jay could tell him he didn't need to know that part of the plan, but that wouldn't be any fun. "Remember that movie with the line, *'If you build it, they will come?'*"

Panda acknowledged with a nod.

"Well, this is *'Field of Fire'* and If you keep a good sight picture, *'they will come,'*" Blue Jay said with a smile.

As the Team members tried to muffle their laughter, Panda went on the attack.

"You know I'm glad JC won the title back. Of course the day isn't over yet. Who knows, he may stop in downtown Baghdad and start directing traffic or piss on one of Big Daddy's statues!" Panda exclaimed as he pointed at Blue Jay.

"How many points would I get for pissing on a statue?" Blue Jay inquired.

"How many points?" Panda echoed, then stated, "I rest my case."

That was a good tension breaker. Everyone, including Panda, still had smiles on their faces as they loaded up and added decals to the vehicles identifying them as Fedayeen.

Between studying maps and using the neat gizmos each vehicle had onboard, getting around downtown Baghdad wasn't very difficult. The uniforms and vehicles had made it undesirable

112

for anyone to challenge or even look in their direction.

The Team took note of Ibn Sina Hospital as their little convoy passed by, then continued a considerable distance before making a left turn onto a side street that ran behind a series of upper class apartment buildings.

When they had driven one block the third vehicle pulled to the curb and stopped. At the next block, the second vehicle went to the curb and the third block the lead vehicle did the same.

The front of the apartment buildings were facing a main thoroughfare while at the rear there were a series of grassy lots. The Oil Intel had made very discreet inquiries about vacant apartments in all of the buildings and passed on the information.

The shooters knew which building and apartment were their objective as they dismounted and walked toward the buildings. The drivers would stay with their vehicles and move them out of the area until needed, but never out of com range of the shooters in the buildings.

Only one pair at a time would make entry into their building with the others staying at ground level for support if needed. So, not to attract additional attention, the three vehicles had moved further down the street and would stay in the immediate area until everyone had made entry, then move on to a more secluded location.

Outdated fire escape systems ran down the back of each building and would be used to make entry.

On Blue Jay's signal Met and Panda moved quietly up the fire escape to the top floor and entered the apartment through a rear window. The two men first checked the apartment to make sure it was vacant then simply said, "In," over the com.

Pru and Benz were next to attempt entry. When the single word, "In," was again heard Blue Jay, Bean, and Jockey proceeded.

The three silently climbed the fire escape, entered the top floor apartment, and checked to make sure it was vacant.

Bean approached Blue Jay and motioned for him to turn off his com unit. That done Bean said, "We may have a problem? There's furniture in the front room."

Blue Jay and Jockey quickly checked the other rooms and

the closets as Bean moved to the door and checked the apartment number.

Bean was informing Blue Jay they had the right apartment as Jockey was rejoining them.

"Only furniture," Blue Jay said thoughtfully. "Are they moving in or moving out? And when will they return?"

"Here's an interesting item I found hanging in the closet," Jockey informed the other two as he held up a white Fedayeen uniform. "Have a feeling this asshole is moving in," Jockey offered.

"Decision time," Blue Jay alerted, "We can abort or stay and take our chances. If either one of you want to abort it's no problem. We'll leave and be in support for the other two shooting teams."

Bean and Jockey looked at each other, shrugged their shoulders and said, "Stay." At that moment Blue Jay switched his com unit back on and said, "In," followed by other words that would alert everyone the apartment might not be vacant and they were staying.

When Blue Jay completed his message the three shooting teams started to set up and the vehicles moved off.

Two men in one of the better hotels in Baghdad were preparing to go out for the evening and were talking about getting lucky with the ladies that evening.

When they completed their preparations they left the hotel. Since they were already in the upscale Al-Mansour district of Baghdad, they decided to walk.

If their Intel was correct and he stuck to his routine, they should see Bedbug at one of two night clubs that evening forcing himself on women.

One of the men was limping and walking with a cane, so their progress was slow.

After looking around for anyone close by the man without the cane asked, "Are you sure you remember which of his legs is dumb from that attempted assassination?"

"Yes," the other reported, "I haven't been out of the business that long."

"Just checking," the man answered then continues with, "Your French is very good."

"Thank you Rene'," the man replied.

"For a Russian," Rene' quickly added and both men smiled.

"Boris," Rene' again asked, "During the Cold War did it ever come to mind that someday you might be working on the same side as someone from the West?"

"Had no time to think of such things," Boris answered, "With the exception of France, I was kept too busy fighting off good Intelligence efforts from the West," and again both men smiled.

Boris and Rene' eventually came to their first stop, had a drink, and then decided to move on.

At the second night club they had better luck. Bedbug was already there trying to force himself on the women, as usual.

Boris and Rene' sat at the bar, ordered two drinks, and pretended to have a conversation. Using mirror reflections, they casually looked around or checked out a female walking past and kept track of every move Bedbug made.

The trick was going to be getting past his bodyguards and within three feet of his bad leg.

An hour had passed when Rene' noticed a large party entering the night club and heading in Bedbugs direction. Rene' made a comment to his partner about the beautiful women in that party. When Boris looked at him after checking out the women, he could tell by the expression on Rene's face what he had in mind.

Rene' already had money out for the tab and placed it on the bar. The two men slid off their stools and took an intercept course to the beautiful women and attached themselves to the end of the group. As the group passed Bedbug, he reached out and grabbed the best beauty in the group and started to make unwanted advances.

With the group blocking the view of one bodyguard and Rene' the other, Boris thought, *'It doesn't get any better than this.'* He raised the cane, pressed it against Bedbugs numb leg, and activated a triggering device that sent a microscopic ball containing the poison ricin into his calf.

That done, Boris continued to excuse himself as he moved slowly through the night club again using the cane to support his injured leg.

The cane was a cousin to an assassination device the KGB developed during the Cold War. It shoots a ball, containing the poison ricin, that could only be seen though a microscope.

Under protest, the KGB was forced to supply the umbrella model of the same device to the Bulgarians who used it to inject ricin into a descendent on London Bridge.

Due to the insistence of the victim's wife, the medical people in London finally found the cause of death after discovering a small puncture in the victim's calf, removing the skin layer by layer and putting it under a microscope until they discovered the ball.

Knowing Bulgarians didn't have the technology or expertise to make such a thing, the finger correctly pointed to the KGB.

CHAPTER SIXTEEN

Blue Jay's cell phone was vibrating. He removed it from his pocket, flipped it open and says. "Yes,"

"Your package is being sent via express." a voice informed him.

"Appreciate it," Blue Jay said and hung up.

Several hours after the phone call the Team heard the sound of many sirens approaching the area and seconds later an ambulance with many escort vehicles pulled into the Ibn Sina Hospital driveway and up to the emergency room entrance. Scopes from three different angles focused in on the ambulance as the back doors were opened. As the patient was rolled out Bean informed Blue Jay, "It's Bedbug."

Blue Jay spoke into the com in a low voice, "Bedbug." Then requested, "Range me."

"1321," Bean replied.

The other shooters and spotters were going through this same routine and the ranges were between 1320 to 1322 yards or approximately three quarters of a mile from the apartment buildings to Ibn Sina Hospital.

While the patient was being wheeled into the emergency room the Team started making additional preparations. The drivers returned with their vehicles and approached the fire escapes. The spotters for each of the shooters were waiting at the top of the fire escapes and lowered a thin black rope they had already secured at their end. The rope was small, but so strong you could use it to hang a Buick upside down.

The men on the ground took their end and temporarily secured it to a place high enough so no one would notice or run into the rope. The three men then retreated to another out of the way place and waited for the next phase.

They didn't have to wait long. Another bunch of sirens could be heard in the distance and everyone was already waiting for whoever it might be.

When a big ass bulletproof limo pulled into the hospital driveway everyone knew it could be Big Daddy and Blue Jay ordered the vehicles to move closer.

Bean was zeroed in on the limo and Jockey's eyes were glued to the little PC screen. The security guards surrounded the vehicle as Big Daddy emerged from the backseat and within a second his big head was filling Bean's scope.

"Turn your head, asshole," Bean muttered.

"That's it, got it," he informed Jockey who had already sent the photo of Big Daddy's ear to the PC for analysis.

The shooters were zeroed in on this guy and ready to shoot, but Blue Jay signaled, "Not good," over the com units and everyone knew a look-alike had showed up to check things out or Big Daddy might have a feeling about something. He was a survivor.

The limo and the surrounding area were being kept under close surveillance when an hour later another limo pulled up.

"Here we go again," Blue Jay alerted the group.

The security people performed the same routine as before then Big Daddy again appeared and Bean was on him. This Big Daddy was more cooperative, the PC performed the analysis and again "Not Good." was heard over the com.

"This ass." But before Blue Jay could say hole he stopped in mid-sentence and instead said, "Someone else is getting out."

"I'm on him," Bean acknowledged.

As another Big Daddy appeared Blue Jay reminded, "The second one, don't lose the second one."

The PC was analyzing the ear and Bean had returned to his spotter duties.

"Range me," Blue Jay again requested.

"1325", Bean replied.

This time it seemed like the PC was taking forever to confirm or reject, but in fact Bean and Jockey were faster this time and the turnaround time was even quicker.

"It's a match," Jockey informed Blue Jay who relayed it into the com unit and within seconds three .50 caliber rounds were traveling toward Big Daddy, one to the head and two to the heart. All three rounds found their mark and all three spotters said, "Target down."

"Climb the wall!" Blue Jay ordered and three semi-automatic rifles started firing at the wall behind the two parked limos. Each round fired was a little higher than the last and gave the impression that they had been fired from a plane making a strafing run. The men continued firing until the ten round rifle magazines were empty.

While the 50s were climbing the wall, Jockey was dialing a number of a cell phone. He didn't know who he was dialing, but knew the message. When the other end answered Jockey said, "Air attack in Baghdad, repeat, air attack in Baghdad." then hung up.

When Gil Dunn got the message from Jockey, he immediately phoned in anonymous tips to major media outlets that Baghdad was under air attack by forces led by exiled Iraqis.

Check was also on a cell phone and dialing the Radio, T.V. and Telecommunication Center in downtown Baghdad. When someone finally answered he reported in a breathless voice, "Planes are shooting up downtown Baghdad," then hung up.

As the shooters and spotters packed up their gear and checked for any spent shell casings, Blue Jay spoke into the com, "Ready."

On that note Check, Tic, and Bris backed their Fedayeen vehicles into the courtyards of the buildings where their shooters were in residence. They retrieved the ropes they temporarily secured earlier and secured them to the back of the vehicles. That done they drove across the courtyard until the rope was taut between them and the apartment windows.

When the shooters and spotters were ready they attached the gizmos to the rope and first the spotters, then the shooters take the ride to the ground just like at the silo back at the Barn, only in the dark.

Panda would be the first to descend and was in position when two men from Baghdad's security force approached Bris and inquired about the vehicle and why he was in the area.

Bris was barely holding his own in the language area when he heard, "Coming through," on his com unit.

Bris was keeping a sharp eye in the area of the black rope and the instant he saw Panda he warned, "Look out!," as he pointed behind the two men.

As the two men turned they were greeted by the bottoms of two boots that knocked them to the ground. Bris and Panda immediately dispatched the two men as Tic then Check arrived on the scene.

"Situation secure," Panda informed everyone on the com and Met started his ride to the ground as one of the security men was loaded into the vehicle.

Everyone was down except Jockey, Bean, and Blue Jay who were in the process.

"Now remember, Jockey, keep your feet together so you don't leave your balls swinging on some unseen tree limb out there in the dark," Bean advised.

"I never liked you," Jockey told Bean as he pushed the thumb brake release and started his journey to the ground. Jockey knew Bean was only kidding, but he kept his feet together anyway.

After Blue Jay made his descent he again spoke into the com. "Arm them," and after a pause ordered, "Do it," and all of the spotters pressed the red button on their device and a small amount of plastique was ignited at one end of the carabineers in each apartment freeing the ropes and allowing them and the carabineers to be pulled down to the vehicles.

With all of the ropes quickly retrieved, packed up, and the second security man loaded into the second vehicle, the Team checked each other's appearance, especially the scarf hiding their faces, and headed out.

Not wanting to get tied up in the mess around the hospital, the three vehicles headed east.

Confusion was starting to grow in the city. The news of Saddam's assassination had not yet spread beyond the Hospital area, but the city is starting to react to reports of an air attack and even parts of Baghdad had gone black.

After dumping the security men into the first body of water they came to, the three vehicles were racing through the streets and under these conditions brought little unwanted attention. Within the city limits were the Fedayeen's primary responsibility and during an emergency they were usually racing to or from somewhere.

With Saddam down and Odai near death, command falls to Qusai who was not as hot-headed as his brother, but much more cunning.

After being notified about his brother's condition earlier in the evening, Qusai ended a meeting he was holding along the Syrian border and was heading back to Baghdad.

When he was told about his father, he was shaken for a few minutes, then recovered and started giving orders.

"I am taking command of everything as of now," he commanded, "Seal the city and put the army on full alert. Get me more details about my father and brother," he then ordered.

———————

As the Team headed for the city limits they came upon a roadblock that seemed to have just been set up by their Fedayeen brothers.

With scarves around their necks and covering half their faces, the Team's com units were totally canceled as Blue Jay said in a low voice, "This may get interesting. Lock and load."

They did not hesitate as they approached, but instead maintained a high rate of speed until they were close to the roadblock then slammed on the brakes, and all three vehicles came to a sliding halt.

Before the people at the roadblock could respond, Check was standing up in the lead vehicle shouting, "Why did you set up your roadblock here? I was instructed to man this location!"

The apparent leader of their group replied with the usual Fedayeen arrogance, but Check held his ground and the words started flying fast and furious as the Team members started selecting their targets in case they were given the word.

In the middle of their argument, the leader ordered Check out of the vehicle and to come closer so they could talk.

Since there was an armored vehicle at the roadblock, Check decided to comply with the order and informed the others what was happening, "I'm going along as a bodyguard," Blue Jay informed everyone then instructed, "Check, make sure we are standing in front of this vehicle when you stop to talk. That will give the Team open fields of fire starting at the front fenders and moving out, if needed."

"Let's do it," Blue Jay ordered and Check, got out, walked to the front of the vehicle and then continued in the direction of the roadblock.

When the two men reached the commander at the roadblock, Blue Jay was standing at Check's right and facing him was a real Fedayeen turd.

It wasn't long before the words were flying fast and furious again. They were talking so fast Blue Jay could only pick up a word here and there, but knew it was getting serious by the look on the man's face in front of him.

He didn't know what Check said on the next exchange of words, but the man standing in front of Blue Jay stepped in Check's direction and pushed him with the weapon he was holding at chest height. Check was pushed off balance and before he could recover Blue Jay connected with a right cross to the jaw of the pusher knocking him out cold.

"That's our cue," Bean said into the com and all three vehicles emptied and took up positions. The formation resembled an Indian arrowhead with the vehicle being the point. If each man fired his automatic weapon the width of his own body, the first burst from the Team would cut a twenty foot wide path threw the opposition.

When Check saw that the leader was trying to keep his troops calm so no further violence would erupt, he went through the same motions.

Since this seemed to have brought their verbal skirmish to an end, the leader at the roadblock recommended they join forces.

Check declined, suggesting too many men would be used for one roadblock and that things might get out of hand with the two groups so close together.

He then informed his counterpart he would move further east and setup his own roadblock.

He and Blue Jay then returned to their group, everyone mounted up, and the three vehicles turned back to the way they had come.

Making a right at the first road they came to, they continued moving east, making turns to the left then right, until they were out of sight of their Fedayeen brothers.

"Nice job," Blue Jay commended Check over the com.

"When in Baghdad do as the Belgium's do," Check replied.

"Maybe I dozed off during that story Pru told us," Jockey informed the others on the com, "but I don't remember the part where the Belgium cold-cocked the SS officer."

"True, true," Blue Jay conceded, "This is the Middle East version of the story. You have to hit some of these fuckers in the face with a hammer just to get their attention."

"Really?" Jockey asked, "Even when his brother is sitting behind him in a halftrack with a cannon pointing at you?"

"Especially then," Blue Jay assured him, then added, "besides, didn't Bean tell you any incoming rounds twenty millimeter and above would be your responsibility?"

"I told him to bring his tennis racket," Bean assured Blue Jay.

"You fuckers from PAW don't listen either, do you?" Blue Jay inquired.

"PAW again," Jockey brooded, "If I made those passes any lower in Corsica the plane would still be in the trees."

"Sorry I missed that, must have been inside," Blue Jay said.

"I was inside too," Bean added.

"I was outside," Check offered, "but missed it. I must have dozed off."

Jockey looked at the three other men then said, "I want to change vehicles."

After clearing the Baghdad city limits the Team turned southeast and were traveling on the main road to Al Kut. At this point in the Project, time and speed were more important than stealth.

———————

Qusai had arrived and was informed that his brother was also dead. That didn't bother him as much as the news about his father. He knew without his father, Uday would have really been

123

out of control and it would only be a matter of time before there was a who kills who first situation or civil war would break out.

Qusai was getting an additional briefing about his father's death and as the group left Ibn Sina Hospital he took note of the bullet holes up the side of the hospital and asked to see the rounds that had been retrieved from the wall.

He then inquired, "Have they been searched?" as he pointed to buildings a few hundred yards away.

"Yes, sir," the senior member of the group reported, "and nothing was found."

Seconds later Qusai was presented with two .50 caliber rounds that had been retrieved from the wall and examined them. Holding the rounds in his right hand he again looked at the wall and inquired, "An air attack was reported. Did anyone see or hear any planes?"

"No sir," the senior man reported, "Just the rounds up the wall and reports from the media."

Qusai thought for a few seconds then commanded, "Search all of these buildings for another mile for anything and get in touch with our media personnel to find out where all of this air attack information came from."

Qusai was still speaking when people started moving in all directions.

The people back in Jersey didn't code name this guy, Slick, for nothing.

Several hours had passed when Qusai put out a country wide alert for any suspicious person or persons to be detained.

Rene' and Boris had already departed on a flight to Syria where they would catch a flight to Greece, then on to Italy and then Switzerland by car, and into retirement for Boris and partial retirement for Rene'. He had decided to give up all activity except his dealings with Gil Dunn.

The Team had already stopped for fuel at a remote filling station and topped off their tanks while Check kept the attendants busy using Fedayeen bully boy tactics until they left the station.

If their luck held they should now have enough fuel for the remainder of the trip.

As they approached Al Kut they saw another roadblock in the distance. Benz was already looking through his spotter scope and reported, "Republican Guard."

"How many?" Blue Jay inquired.

"I count fifteen," Benz reported.

"Well, its daylight, we're outside of Baghdad, and in their territory," Blue Jay stated his feelings over the com, "If we try to push our way through like last time, they might push back. I also have to wonder why this roadblock is setup and if the orders came from Baghdad." "Unless anyone has a good alternative, I say we blow through these guys before they have us cold."

When there were no alternatives offered Bean inquired, "How do you want to do this?"

"Very carefully," Blue Jay stated, then continued with the plan as they moved toward the roadblock.

The three vehicle convoy were moving fast as they approached then began to slow down.

When they were close to the truck blocking the road Check stood up in the vehicle and yelled, "No brakes, no brakes," as Bean pretended he is pumping the brake pedal.

The men at the roadblock saw the other two vehicles were stopping and assumed the first one had really lost their brakes.

To avoid a crash Bean steered toward the rear of the truck and as he passed behind it Blue Jay tossed a grenade into the back.

Bean sped up, turned to the left, stopped the vehicle, and everyone bailed out then used the right side of the vehicle for cover.

When the soldiers saw everyone bailing out they brought their weapons up to the ready, but the grenade exploding followed by automatic weapons fired from the four men behind the vehicle stopped any threat of an assault.

Tic pressed the gas pedal to the floor and followed the path Bean took while Bris held his position as everyone dismounted and took cover around the vehicle.

When Tic broke through the smoke coming from the truck

everyone opened fire on the Republican Guard troops. Some returned fire and were cut down by the seven men in the two vehicles. Others tried to seek cover behind the burning truck and were dispatched by automatic weapons fire from the third vehicle.

When opposition fire stopped fifteen men were dead or wounded and Blue Jay whispered, "Back into the vehicles," into the com followed by Check yelling the same thing in Iraqi to keep the hoax going.

The men mounted up and the Team was again on their way.

After passing through Al Kut the Team stopped, changed into desert camies and buried the black suits.

Plan A was to use the black Fedayeen suits as cover and travel the main road through Al Kut, Al Amarah, and Al Basrah to the Persian Gulf or Kuwait.

Plan B was to travel the main road to its closest point to the Iranian border then head for Iran.

With Plan B now in effect Jockey was on the radio back to home base, alerting them about the change in plans, and giving them the coordinates for the contact.

That done the Team was again on the road.

CHAPTER SEVENTEEN

The cargo plane had been gassed up and additional ammunition, water, and supplies had been put on board in case Plan B was activated or for any other unforeseen situations.

JC was preparing to leave, but was having second thoughts about taking Mac due to the danger factor.

"Mac, do you want to sit this one out?" JC offered. "Once in and out of Iran airspace was okay, but to do it twice in a two-day period is pushing our luck.

"Plus the AWAC's planes probably eyeballed us during the entire first trip and will be really watching this time."

"You know, you're right, maybe I should skip this one," Mac agreed.

"Are you serious?" JJ asked. "If you are I think it's a good decision."

"No, I'm not serious, ass wipe," Mac snapped at JJ.

"Take this pecker head with you," JJ urged, "maybe he'll run into that gangster Charley Tuna and get my high priced-weapons back."

"Him and those fucking weapons," Mac declared, "will it ever end?"

"We better get," JC recommended as he turned and walked toward the cargo plane.

JC and Mac had taken the same route when leaving Kuwait and continued out over the Persian Gulf, but instead of entering Iran and using the mountain ranges for concealment, they were staying close to the Iran/Iraq border and a more direct line to the pick-up coordinates.

"Mac, keep a sharp eye on how close we are to Iraq," JC requested, "I want to stay out of sight of the border, but don't want to stray too far into Iran."

"No problem," Mac assured JC as they passed over the Karun River east of Al Basrah in Iraq.

Since plan B was now in effect, the closest the main road came to the Iranian border was between Al Kut and Ai Amarah where the road direction changes from east to south east. According to the locator gizmos the Team was in the area where the road came closest to the Iran border and the vehicles reduced their speed. They hadn't passed any other vehicles coming from the other direction for a while and no one was behind them.

The three vehicles moved slowly looking for a road the map said was there and stopped when they came upon a sub-standard secondary road that headed east.

'This must be it,' Blue Jay reasoned and instructed the lead vehicle to turn onto the road followed by the other two.

"The border should be about fifteen miles ahead," he then informed the others.

When the Team was approximately two miles from the border they saw two Iranian jet fighters pursuing a lumbering cargo plane.

The aircraft was ordered to land and JC had been stalling for time as he headed for Iraqi airspace, but time had run out and the lead jet had fired a warning burst in front of the plane.

Continuing this effort JC was going through the motions of landing by dropping to a lower altitude and faking an approach as Mac kept feeding him updated locations.

"It's going to be close," JC alerted Mac.

One of the U.S. AWACS had been tracking the three planes when they started heading toward the border, had vectored two F-16's to the area, and they were on patrol overhead.

"This is going to be interesting," Blue Jay suggested, "The plane is in a country illegally with their air force in hot pursuit while they are trying to get into a neighboring country illegally where the U.S. has fighters on patrol."

"Boggles the mind doesn't it?" Bean offered.

The Iranian fighters realized what the plane was trying to do and the lead plane made a wide sweep and was approaching from the right side.

"I think this guy coming in from the right is getting serious." Mac informed JC.

"How close to the border?" JC inquired.

"One mile," Mac replied.

JC checked his speed and altitude then stayed straight and level while he watched the jet make its approach.

"He's making himself a sitting duck isn't he?" Blue Jay asked Jockey.

"He figures coalition fighters are on patrol in the area by now," Jockey answered.

"But he is still in Iran and this fighter is going to shoot him down," Blue Jay offered.

"I wouldn't count on it," Jockey said with a smile. "This guy has balls of steel."

The Iranian jet took an angle so he would be able to take out the flight deck. If it crashed in Iraq who cared, it was shot down in Iranian airspace.

JC and Mac kept a close watch on the jet. He wasn't moving supersonic for this pass on a lumbering duck, so it made it easier to keep track of him.

The jet was heading straight for them and JC continued to fly straight and normal.

"Anytime you want to do your pilot shit," Mac suggested.

As the jet pilot put his finger on the trigger, JC pushed the wheel forward and pulled on the air breaks. The forward airspeed immediately dropped and the aircraft rapidly lost altitude.

The jet saw what was happening and fired a burst as he tried to change his angle of attack, but was too close.

Mac watched as several tracer rounds passed above the flight deck.

"How far?" JC again requested.

"Welcome to Iraq," Mac replied, "but I'd say that Iranian is pissed and we are in the middle of a whole lot of nowhere."

"Help should be here soon," JC reassured Mac.

As JC was answering Mac the F-16's were challenging the Iranian fighters who seemed to be ignoring them. As the lead F-

16 kept challenging the second one was requesting instructions from command headquarters.

JC was hugging the deck knowing it made for a harder target as the Iranian swung around for another pass.

"Any word yet?" the lead F-16 inquired.

"Nothing."

"Figures."

"Doesn't that fighter look a little dirty to you?" the lead F-16 inquired.

"Why yes it does," the other pilot replied then added, "I'll go see if the other one is in the same condition."

Seconds later the F-16's broke formation and the lead headed for the Iranian that was setting up on the cargo plane.

The Iranian would make sure he didn't miss this time as he closed in for the kill, but was again disappointed when the lead F-16 approached him at a forty-five-degree angle and passed in front of him causing the Iranian to fly through the F-16's jet wash. This could cause a jet to lose control and crash if the pilot wasn't good enough to deal with it.

The second Iranian saw the maneuver and gave pursuit to the U.S. plane, but immediately found himself in missile lock.

"Do you really want to do that?" the second F-16 pilot inquired out loud as he maintained perfect firing position.

With one fighter in missile lock and the other shaken up by the jet wash, the two planes decided to return home.

As the F-16's made sure the planes were returning to Iran, they instructed the cargo plane they would be escorted to the nearest airfield to land.

Without replying JC circled then came in for a landing.

The Team was again wearing the masks they used when they jumped the border into Iraq.

The F-16's couldn't patrol overhead forever, but they could get pictures as they made passes over the landed aircraft and the three vehicles not far away.

The Photo Interrupters would analyze the pictures, report the Iranian markings on the plane, and that the vehicles were Iraqi Fedayeen.

Some analyst in Washington, D.C. would say it looked like a

high-level Iranian defections to Iraq or an Iraqi spy fleeing back home.

Objections from the field saying, 'It looked more involved than that,' would be over ruled by some genius in D.C..

The three vehicles moved close to the plane and JC lowered the rear ramp. Everyone entered the plane and discussed their options as the F-16's continued their slow passes.

"Well we can't fly out," JC informed everyone. "We wouldn't be able to shake AWAC's, so Iraqi airspace is out and those people over there must be really pissed and will be watching very closely."

"How is your situation?" JC then inquired.

"Can't say for sure," Blue Jay replied, "things were going very well until we ran into a roadblock about one hundred miles from Baghdad. It may be just a coincidence or maybe someone in Baghdad is thinking."

"Slick?" JC inquired.

"That would be my guess," Blue Jay answered, "By now he's the main man."

"It looks like we'll be motoring out of Iraq," JC said, "and thanks to Mac, who insisted on being prepared for anything, we are in good shape. We have selected goodies onboard consisting of food, water, ammo, fuel, C-4 and detonators."

"The next question is should we move quickly or find a remote site hold up for a day or two then move out?" JC stated.

"Between the shootout at the roadblock and this incident, which will probably be on CNN in no time, Slick will probably flood this area with troops on a search and destroy mission," Blue Jay offered, "If Slick is not calling the shots, holding up would be better."

"Good points," JC agreed, "We can't run the risk Slick is not running the show. Are those F-16's still out there?"

"Think they called it a day," Jockey replied.

"Let's load up and prepare to move out," JC ordered.

When everything was loaded, JC went to vehicle two and Mac to three for the ride to Kuwait. As Mac approached his ride he looked up to see Bris behind the wheel. "Maceee," Bris greeted Mac.

"Not you," Mac pleaded as he looked around and then saw Panda already seated, "and this one too? No, no this won't do," Mac announced.

"Want to change?" JC offered.

"That's okay," Mac declined, "Maybe I'll be able to get these heathens under control during the trip back?"

The three loaded vehicles moved a good distance from the plane and stopped. It must be destroyed to get rid of any telltale evidence. JC produced a remote detonator, armed it, pressed the red button, and the cargo plane exploded causing a ball of fire.

"There seems to be a pattern developing," Panda observed, "If he can't get them to crash he blows them up."

Between being cautious and avoiding fire fights, it took five days for the Team to arrive at the Iraq/Kuwait border.

Blue Jay had kept in touch by radio with Gil Dunn and he would have two Hummers waiting at the place they planned to cross the border.

Since they couldn't drive the Fedayeen vehicles outside of Iraq, they would be burned out and abandoned just prior to the border crossing.

The .50 caliber's and the Remington light weight Bean was carrying were too big to conceal and would have to be disassembled and the parts buried in the desert at different locations. Mac was already working on a story for JJ about that part.

The MP-5's and 9mm Bereta's could be carried under their camies and would be kept.

It would be good to be back in friendly territory again, but for security reasons the Team still had to stay unknown to the military and local police.

―――――――――

With all of the preparations completed the Team was making the crossing into Kuwait. Using their night vision gear and com units, they were able to side-step smugglers and whoever else was crossing illegally.

Once they were in Kuwait they walked to where the

Hummers were waiting. John Howard, Jeff Dawson, Charles Wilson, Gil Dunn, and Foxie delivered the Hummers earlier and were keeping watch at a distance.

"Are you sure we have the right place?" John Howard inquired.

"They'll be here," Dunn assured him.

"They already are," Foxie corrected, as he stared into the darkness around the vehicles.

With that everyone looked harder and a few seconds later could see movement around the two Hummers.

"Foxie, you certainly have good night vision," John remarked.

"Just takes practice," Foxie replied with a smile. Not knowing the Board had been keeping the Hummers secure, the Team ran their usual security checks. When they were satisfied they loaded up and headed out for the remote airfield where JJ, Top and the Ladies were waiting.

"Due to security reasons, I guess this will be the closest we ever get to meeting the Team," Charley Wilson said as the Hummers drove off.

"We all know Blue Jay, but none of the others," Jeff Dawson added then asked, "Do you know any of the others, Gil?"

"Just Bean," Dunn answered, as he turned the key to start the engine. "He and Blue Jay used to work for me at the Agency."

"Maybe we should change that rule?" Howard suggested.

"Or at least bring it up for discussion at the next board meeting," Wilson recommended.

The Board kept discussing the issue as Gil started the drive back to their hotel.

I guess JJ would have another mutiny on his hands at the next Board meeting.

CHAPTER EIGHTEEN

The sun was still trying to climb over the horizon to start the next day, but it was light enough to see a good distance.

The four remaining at the airfield had been standing two-hour guard shifts each night and Top was on the last fifteen minutes of his shift.

The group had been maintaining surveillance in the area, using binoculars and range finders for more distant surveillance.

JJ was the first up and noticed Top was looking very intently into a pair of binoculars. Not wanting to scare him JJ just walked up beside him and stood there looking out where Top was focused.

"We may be getting company," Top alerted JJ.

"I wonder if they're friend or foe," JJ inquired.

"The latter," Top answered, "they look like more of those turds that stopped by here the last time."

"I'll wake the Ladies," JJ volunteered.

Top, Lady1 and LadyA had brought their favorite weapons for this type of terrain. The Ladies had M-1 carbines and Top favored the M-14 rifle for three to five hundred yard shooting.

JJ could also shoot the rifle, but favored the pistol these days. "How do we know for sure they are the enemy and not just wonders?" JJ inquired.

"Well, it's daylight so we can't sneak up on them and listen. None of us speak their lingo, so I guess it's the Navy way," Top answered then added, "did I say Navy?" and jokingly spit several times to get the taste out of his mouth.

"I'll get setup and fire a shot across their bow," Top said. "If they keep coming, another shot. After the third shot I'd say they are serious about coming in."

JJ agreed with Top. Besides, if they got in too close they could overwhelm the four of them.

Top and the Ladies were setting up as JJ kept looking at the approaching jeeps through the binoculars.

"I have a feeling about this," JJ informed the others. "There are three in each jeep and in this part of the world they usually travel with a full house."

When Top had the windage and elevation set on his M-14 he asked,

"Everyone ready?"

"Ready," the Ladies answered.

"Think I'll stand here and observe for a while," JJ informed Top. "I'm better with this anyway," he said and raised a 9mm Bretta pistol.

"No problem," Top replied, "First across the bow shot going out."

Several seconds later a round was kicking up the sand in front of the two advancing jeeps. They first came to a halt, but then continued. The second round landed a little closer to the lead jeep, but this time it didn't even slow down.

"Maybe he thinks your not serious," LadyA inquired.

"Yeah, put one into his front fender," Lady1 suggested.

"It will probably make him show his real intentions," JJ agreed.

Top took aim and fired the third shot hitting the right front fender. The sound could still be heard when both jeeps picked up speed and machine gun fire from the second jeep started hitting the hangar.

"Hit the fender!" Top said out loud, as he took aim at the man firing the automatic weapon.

Lady1 and LadyA focused on the other jeep as it took a more direct course toward the hangar.

The Ladies took up the slack in their trigger squeeze, and one then two rounds were speeding toward the jeep's windshield followed by several more in rapid succession.

Top's jeep was moving parallel to the hangar and he was right with it. Then the M-14 spoke and the man with the automatic was thrown out the side of the jeep.

With so many rounds coming through the windshield the other jeep tried to turn away, but it was too late. First the passenger then the driver were taken out and the man in the back bailed out and took cover behind the jeep after it came to a halt.

Top took out the driver in his jeep then the passenger in quick succession.

The man taking cover behind the jeep had an automatic weapon, but he was not firing at the hangar. *'Maybe he's scared or maybe it's something else,'* JJ thought to himself, as he took a step forward putting himself outside the hangar doors.

From his position Top was checking the downed enemy.

The Ladies were focusing on what the guy behind the jeep had in mind, when another gunman appeared from their side of the hangar and brought his weapon to bear, but two rounds from a 9mm Bretta stopped his motion. After firing, JJ turned to his left and fired two more rounds into another man as soon as he appeared from that side of the hangar.

The man behind the jeep saw what had just happened and started to flee.

The Ladies were distracted for a few seconds, then two rounds from M-1 carbines took down the running gunman.

When all was quiet again the four people waited to see if any other action was going to break out.

———————

It was afternoon by the time the Team arrived at the airfield and they were surprised when they saw the six bodies and two jeeps close to the hangar.

Not seeing anyone around the two Hummers stopped abruptly and everyone was out in a flash with weapons at the ready. Spreading out they moved on the hangar ready for a fire fight at the drop of a hat. As they moved into the hangar and around the jet they saw JJ, Top, Lady1, then LadyA and were relieved everyone was all right.

"The cavalry has arrived," Top announced.

"Didn't you know the cavalry are supposed to arrive in the nick of time to save us all?" LadyA advised.

"Not if you're stuck with F Troop," Lady1 corrected.

"It looks like the House three, the Team zero," JJ calculated.

"It seems like we had a lot of misplaced concern," Blue Jay advised his people as they all broke into laughter.

"Let's dump those bodies, police up the empty shell casings and any other things lying around," JC ordered, "The Hummers will be picked up by the Oil Intel so we'll park them in the hangar after the jet backs out."

"Jockey, let's you and I check the jet for any problem bullet holes."

People were moving in all directions as the orders are being carried out.

One hour later the jet was backed out of the hangar and replaced by the two Hummers.

Everyone was on the plane except JC and Blue Jay who were waiting for the drivers of the Hummers to board the jet.

Check and Tic approached the plane and continued up the boarding stairs.

With everyone on the plane Blue Jay looked at JC and said,

"Well, we survived another one."

"Looks that way," JC confirmed.

"Did you ever have any doubts about this one?" Blue Jay inquired.

"None at all," JC announced in a loud voice.

"You're full of shit," Blue Jay announced in an equally loud voice. "Going into a strange country to take out the top people with a group this size."

Everyone on the plane could hear the commotion and looked out the side windows.

"We aren't even off the ground and it's starting already," Panda observed.

When the two men finally boarded the jet, Panda inquired,

"Blue Jay, did the Bull Shit Derby start already?"

"No, but if anyone has to get off the plane, wipe your feet before getting back on because there is a whole bunch of horse shit at the bottom of the stairs."

"Blue Jay, Bubbie," JC pleaded while in the middle of roaring laughter.

"Shall we?" Air Jockey inquired to JC as his laughter subsided.

JC joined Jockey and minutes later the jet was rolling down the airstrip then jumped into the air. The jet was flying low until they were out over the Persian Gulf when Jockey pulled it to a reasonable altitude.

As things settled into a normal flight JJ said, "Just remembered, I didn't see the .50 caliber rifles. Are they on board?"

"Sure they are," Mac reassured him.

"Are you sure? I don't remember seeing them," JJ insisted. "Well, if you would stop shooting people you would remember these things," Mac told him.

"Met, Pru, are the fifties on board?" JJ inquired again.

"I know nothing," Met answered with a heavy German accent.

"Okay, what's the story?" JJ interrogated Mac.

"Well, I didn't want to get you upset, but we gave them to a mobster named Sunny Sands for helping us through the mine fields, I mean desert."

JJ looked at Mac and asked, "Isn't the mine field one of stories from the last time two fifties went missing and you told me the mobster, Charley Tuna, helped the Team in Cuba?"

"Well yeah, it could be," Mac confessed. "I get confused."

"I'll confuse you," JJ said as he got Mac in a headlock and both men broke into laughter.

Panda was looking out the side window and announced, "And as we leave this trouble-free paradise we say, what do we say?" Panda inquired, and everyone offered their suggestions.

Finally able to relax, everyone on the plane caught up on some Z's as Jockey and JC took turns piloting the jet back to Mercer Field in Jersey.

———————

Once again everyone was enjoying the after Project dinner and after having had their fill, most were on their second cup of coffee and feeling peaceful.

"JJ, will you answer a question for me?" Jockey asked.

"If I can," JJ answered.

"We went into Baghdad and straight to the apartment buildings across from that hospital and set up the triangulation of fire. How did you know Big Daddy would show up there?"

"I can tell you part of the reason," JJ started.

"As you know it was the Ibn Sina Hospital and it is for VIP's. As a matter of fact, when Bedbug was shot up in his car during an assassination attempt, he was taken to Ibn Sina Hospital."

"I can't go into details about the next part, so let's just say arrangements were made to make sure that Bedbug would require some serious hospital time. He would be in a bad way and only get worse."

"With one of his two sons in critical condition and moving toward death, we figured there was a strong possibility Big Daddy would eventually show up."

"How could you be so sure this VIP hospital wouldn't save him?" Bris inquired.

"The poison used was Ricin and before anyone would figure it out, he would be dead after lingering unpleasantly, then in a coma. In addition to taking out Bedbug we made sure Al Quaida was brought under suspicion in Iraq since they seem to be all over CNN about working with and storing up Ricin."

When it seemed the serious stuff had ended, Panda decided it was time to start the Bull Shit Derby.

"So JJ," he inquired, "I hope it didn't come to hand-to-hand combat with those people that attacked the hangar in our absence?"

"No," JJ assured Panda, "but two of them did get a little close."

"Happy to hear that," Panda said. "I know how the Ladies can get with those stilettos. Those men would be in paradise with seven virgins each and no tools."

"You keep saying that," LadyA scolded. "We didn't do anything to those men in D.C.. We just wanted to scare them."

"You did a good job," Jockey admitted, "I'll bet they're still running."

"Well, if people would show up on time we wouldn't have to

worry about hand-to-hand combat," LadyA made her entry into the Derby.

"Like I said, It's F Troop," Lady1 added. "If we fired a cannon every morning before we raised the flag, the Barn would look like Swiss cheese."

"The cavalry is supposed to arrive in time to save the day," Top offered followed by Lady1's, "It's F Troop."

Top, Lady1, and LadyA always enjoyed listening to the Derby and were really enjoying being active participants.

It finally quieted down and was Air Jockey's turn to stir things up. "I'm sure you are all wondering about the current standings in the annual JC Crazy Fuck Award."

"We had three serious contenders until the panel revisited entries for Benz and disallowed one of them."

"They decided that almost causing a major shootout with the terrorist, Al-Shehih, in the parking lot of a fast food restaurant would be allowed."

"However, talking about the mother of a giant man holding a big knife just to get him to attack so he could throw him off a cliff, will not be allowed."

"Who are these panel members," Benz asked with a smile.

"It's a secret," Jockey replied, "Not even I know their identities." Then added, "And that leaves us with two entries, Blue Jay and JC."

"JC, whose name graces the award," Jockey motioned toward JC and he acknowledged the mock applause, "was way out in front with his, I can land this plane as hard as I want, anywhere I want, and who gives a shit if the explosives go off, until Blue Jay took the lead with the maneuver called, I'm going backward and if that tractor trailer doesn't stop in a straight line it will crush me and this little Porsche." Jockey again stopped to allow more mock applause.

"After that it got fast and furious," Jockey said, "JC made a comeback with his, You can't hit me with those rounds, I'm standing sideways, as he confronted a group of bandits in Kuwait and followed by let's see if we can scratch the undercarriage of this plane on that mountain.

"Blue Jay yet again took the lead when he cold-cocked a

member of a Fedayeen roadblock, in the middle of Iraq, even though the man was backed up by a group with a big cannon."

"But JC would not be denied and returned to his strong point and the, we should maneuver right now so that Iraqi fighter doesn't shoot us down, but let's wait a little longer and is now ahead on points.

"Mac was voted honorable mention in both plane incidents for being in the co-pilot seat and was awarded half a point," Jockey finished the report.

"Will that be half a point for each episode?" Mac inquired. "Half a point total," Jockey answered.

"This award shit is fixed," Mac complained.

Jockey raised his hand and again is speaking, "Something else has just come to mind. While reviewing these episodes, I suggest we may want to add a nut doctor to staff for some individuals."

"The man from Pussy Airways speaks," JC observed.

"He speaks again and again," Blue Jay added.

LadyA raised her hand then offered, "I suggest we change the name from Pussy Airways to Puss Puss Airways."

"Puss Puss Airways," JC repeated the suggestion. "I like it."

"How about a little help over here?" Jockey requested to Panda.

"Don't want to piss off the Ladies," Panda replied, "I want to keep all of my parts intact."

Noticing the Bull Shit Derby was getting far too organized and civilized with all of the hand raising and taking turns to speak, Pru decided to make an entry,

"I say Top," he started, "since the long guns always seem to get the primary target on these Projects, don't you think we deserve points?"

"More than a few I'd say," Met added to kick things up a notch.

That question brought the Team to complete silence and they again prepared for their verbal attacks on the shooters, but Top's answer cut them off when he said, "I've always said that and feel the Ladies and myself should also get points, but the Team seems to take all of the credit."

"Yeah, the F Troop," Lady1 and LadyA both added.

"Didn't see that one coming," Pru confided to Met. "This is jolly good. So much for organized and civilized."

With new blood in the Derby the Team was having a ball. It was not the Team against the House Team, it's more like everybody against everybody else.

When they were all still going strong into the second hour, JJ asked Mac, "Do you think this Derby will come to an end before the next Project?"

"I'm sure it will," Mac answered. "I may be wrong, but I think we may need to get new fifties."

JJ looked at Mac and asked, "You think that's funny don't you?"

"No!" Mac pleaded with a big smile on his face. "Does it look like I think it's funny?"

"Seriously, Mac," JJ said. "What happened to those other fifties? I figure Sunny Sands means you buried the weapons in the sunny desert, but what does Charley Tuna mean?"

Mac paused before answering, then shared the answer with JJ.

The Bull Shit Derby was brought to a complete halt when everyone heard JJ's exploding voice saying, "They threw them into the fucking ocean!! They weren't even supposed to be on a boat."

"Fuck a mine field!" Blue Jay relayed to Bean in a low voice.

A few hours later the Derby had finally ran out of gas and the Team had decided to call it a night. JC and Blue Jay are the first to leave the house and are en route to the Barn when they both pause to light up cigars. The remainder of the Team continued on with Panda and Jockey bringing up the rear.

"This isn't good," Panda observed.

"I know," Jockey added, "When they are alone it's bad enough, but together who knows what mayhem may break out."

"He wants to arm wrestle me for the Award," JC replied as

he continued lighting his cigar.

Jockey and Panda give out a laugh as they continued on to the Barn.

"I think the reasons for the award are partly out of concern for our well being and partly for humor, but humor seems to always get the upper hand." Blue Jay observed.

"Tell me about it," JC agreed with a chuckle.

"I wonder how that award committee got formed?" JC inquired.

"I think it was around the time you made the announcement that Jockey learned to fly at Pussy Airways," Blue Jay replied

"I believe your right," JC agreed with a hearty laugh.

"What a good group," JC said with pride.

"And they think the world of you," Blue Jay confirmed.

"Good to hear," JC acknowledged.

"Ya know for someone that claimed to be too long in the tooth to lead the team in the field, you seem to be out front a lot," Blue Jay observed.

"Look who's talking," JC replied, "you didn't get into the award race for nothing."

"Well you see, when I was in the Corps I had this commanding officer like that and it must have rubbed off."

Blue Jay replied, "As a matter of fact he was still being awarded Purple Hearts when he was a Major."

"Like General Longstreet said, 'You can't lead from behind'," JC answered.

"So we are going to tell Jockey it's General Longstreets' fault we are out front so much?" Blue Jay inquired.

"Works for me," JC agreed.

The two men decided to walk down the long lane to the main road while they smoked their cigars. A full moon is so bright it seemed more like afternoon then after midnight. When the two reached the end of the lane they leaned against the gate and took in the view across the fields.

"We have come a long way in a short time with this group," Blue Jay observed.

"A very short time," JC agreed.

"How long will you be staying with the Projects," Blue Jay

inquired.

"That's a good question," JC answered, "probably wouldn't be involved at all if the government had a handle on what was going on. Unfortunately between the bureaucrats, the politicians and just plain incompetence they can't seem to get a handle on this new type of warfare, so I'll do what I can until they do."

"How about yourself," JC inquired.

"Feel about the same way and have to agree with your reasoning," Blue Jay replied, "have heard about FBI field agents developing sources or Intel about Al-Qaida only to be put down by management in Washington." "You have to wonder how many lives would have been spared if it wasn't for the bureaucrats."

"It is a sad situation," JC agreed. "Well our little group will continue taking out some of those terrorist groups. That should prevent some innocent lives from being lost."

"I wonder where the next project will take us?" Blue Jay wondered out loud.

The two men continued their conversation as the smoke from their two cigars swirled up overhead and merged with the bright moon light.

www.ingramcontent.com/pod-product-compliance
Lightning Source LLC
Chambersburg PA
CBHW020136180626
46810CB00004B/1588